THE GRANDFATHERS SPEAK

Other Titles in the Series

THE GRANDFATHERS SPEAK

Native American Folk Tales of
the Lenapé People

Collected and written by

Hìtakonanu'laxk (Tree Beard)

INTERLINK BOOKS
NEW YORK

First published in 1994 by

INTERLINK BOOKS
An imprint of Interlink Publishing Group, Inc.
99 Seventh Avenue
Brooklyn, New York 11215

Library of Congress Cataloging-in-Publication Data

Hïtakonanu'laxk.
The grandfathers speak : native American folk tales of the
Lenapé people / collected and written by Hïtakonanu'laxk
(Tree Beard).
p. cm. — (International folk tales)
ISBN 1–56656–129–9 — ISBN 1–56656–128–0 (pbk.)
1. Delaware Indians—Legends. 2. Delaware Indians—History.
I. Title. II. Series.
E99.D2H73   1994
973'.04973 — dc20   93–39771
                                              CIP

Printed and bound in the United States of America

10 9 8 7 6 5 4 3 2 1

To my wife, Ginny, for her support and without whom this book would not have been possible. To the memories of my Great-Great-Grandmother, Tonnia, and my Grandfather, James Chamberlain; and to my father, Uncle Clarence and my Aunt Sarah, for their inspiration and for instilling within me a pride in my Native heritage.

PRONUNCIATION GUIDE

This is a guide to be used to help the reader pronounce the Lenapé words that appear throughout this book. The Lenapé (Delaware) language used is the Old Tongue, spoken in Pennsylvania and Ohio in the eighteenth century. Although different in some respects, it is not too dissimilar from modern Unami-Oklahoma dialect.

Vowel Sounds

Lenapé	Sound in English
a	**ah** as in **father** (long)
à	**uh** as in **but** (short)
e	**ay** as in **lay** (long)
è	**eh** as in **let** (short)
i	**ee** as in **see** (long)
ì	**ih** as in **bit** (short)
o	**oh** as in **so** (long)
â or ò	**aw** as in **law** (short)
u	as in **boot** (long)
ù	as in **foot** (short)

Consonants

Lenapé	Sound in English
b	b
ch	ch
d	d
h	h
j	zsh (like z followed by sh — no English equivalent)
k	k (not pronounced too hard)
l	l at beginning of words, or in the middle of a word before a vowel; voiceless at the end of a word (say **lot** without any vibration of vocal cords).
m	m
n	n
p	p
s	fth sound in middle of a word. s sound at beginning of

a word.

s or z sound at the end
of a word.

sh	**sh**
t	**t**
w	**w**
x	No English equivalent; like **ch** in Scottish **loch** — guttural.
z	**z**

CONTENTS

THE GRANDFATHERS SPEAK

INTRODUCTION

The stories, tales and legends to be found within the pages of this book are those of my Lenapé (Delaware) Indian ancestors, n'Lenape'wák, my People. Many of these are not to be found in books at the local bookstore or public library. For much of this literature remains unknown and has long lain forgotten in private collections, in the works of the eighteenth century Moravian missionaries, and the Smithsonian archives, among others. It is sad, but unfortunately true, that much that lies herein has been forgotten, even among my own people. However, other stories have been more fortunate, escaping the alienation that has occurred between my people and their traditions, language, spirituality, and culture. These tales have been handed down and kept alive on the tongues of our elders and storytellers. It is here that I thank them and honor them for the work they do.

Most of the literature presented here is told just as it was long ago, and I am honored to bring these stories all together in print for the first time. In sharing it with you here may these pages also honor my ancestors and my people.

Many of the stories which can be found in old books and publications, such as the Lenapé creation story, exist in those sources in abbreviated forms or are very much changed compared with the original story content. I have presented these in their entirety within these pages. There were others that had to be reconstructed, as parts of those stories were missing, and so I went to other Algonquin sources—Cree, Ojibwe, etc.—to make them as close to their original tellings as possible. In many instances our Lenapé stories will be found to be similar to the stories of our other Algonquin relatives—the Crees, Abnaki, Shawnee, Ojibwe, Micmac, Sauk, Fox, Potawatomi, etc. This is not surprising, however, as the Lenapé were considered to be

1

the progenitors, the Grandfathers of all the Algonquin peoples. One reason that prompted me to search out and write down the stories of my Lenapé people, was that I was unable to find them in the available literature. There was material to be found on many of the Native American peoples, but most of it seemed to be concerned with the Lakota (Sioux). Hardly anything was to be found on the stories of my ancestors, my Lenapé (Delaware) people.

My Lenape'wàk, Lenapé people, have a rich and varied storytelling tradition and it is hoped that through the efforts of this book others may come to know our stories, and in so doing come to know something of my people, our customs and traditions, and our relationship with our original home of the eastern woodlands.

OUR SPIRITUAL VIEW OF THE LAND

Lenape'hokink, Land of the Lenapé, the original homeland of my people, encompasses what is now southeastern New York, the New York City and Hudson River area, and the states of Delaware, New Jersey and eastern Pennsylvania. This is the land of my people, as it was given to us long ago by the Creator. Though it has been occupied and claimed for two hundred years by the United States, it is still our land, and we Lenapé are still here today; we never left.

Our concept of land is that it is not a thing to be possessed, but rather something sacred and alive. We have a saying, "We do not own the land, we are of the land, we belong to it." We call the Earth, Kukna, our mother. All life comes from the Earth, she nourishes us, carries all life and gives us a place to put our feet.

Our belief is that different peoples were given different lands upon which to live, and different religions and ceremonies, to keep the Earth and all life in proper balance and in harmony. The Creator set a pattern here, there is a reason for everything as it was set forth, even people and where they live. Our Creator, he made no mistakes. It is not much different than if one considers the heart being where it is in the body and not in the head where the brain is. The heart is where it is for a reason, and this can also be said of a people. The function of the heart in the body is analagous to the religion and ceremonies of a people. Our spirituality, our religion, is our heartbeat, and our culture and traditions, our life's blood.

We, the eastern Lenapé people, are like a heartbeat in our lands of Lenape'hokink, for we are of this land and we are the land. Each generation is here but for a little while, and while we are alive, it is our responsibility to see that the land remains pure and undefiled, so that our future generations may continue to live here in health and happiness. What we do to the land, to the Earth, we do to ourselves and those of the future generations yet unborn.

There is no separation between a people and the land upon which they live. Men and women are but a part of the greater circle of life, and not superior to it in any way. We are dependent on everything for our very lives. Without the rocks and minerals, without the plants, the trees and the animals, we couldn't live. Indeed, there is much in the land to cause us to be thankful and to be humble.

We are meant to live close to the Earth and all life, interacting in dependence upon it for our very lives. We were meant to live from the Earth, hunting and growing our food—this the Creator gave us as our life's plan long ago, part of his original instruction to us. Modern people have forgotten their instructions, forgotten their connection to the land, to life. Our growing populations, our whole way of life is out of balance and threatens all life upon the Earth.

No longer do we drink the water from where we live. Water now usually comes from a distant reservoir and is treated with chemicals. So, we take it for granted, not really knowing it or understanding it, and we have become out of touch with its spirit. No longer hunting or growing our food, we no longer know our place in the circle of life, and we fail to understand the natural world around us.

We have now surrounded ourselves with a world of our own making, one that is artificial and against life. A world where things are more important than people, or animals, trees or plants, and where roads, industry, and housing developments take precedence over a beautiful untouched piece of land, unspoiled and of pristine beauty. Such a world can only result in death, of our future generations and perhaps all life. There is much that is wrong in the land today, and as long as we continue to live apart from it, out of touch with the soil, the rain, the sun, and nature, our society will be out of touch with ourselves, with each other, and we will leave behind all sorts of problems for the generations yet to come. We will not be the ones who will ultimately be affected by our actions, but it is our children and their children that will suffer.

We can't keep cutting down the trees, polluting the water and the Earth, and continue living for today without thinking of tomorrow. Some call human achievement progress, but we are progressing ourselves right into extinction and perhaps all life along with us! We Lenapé hope that our prophecies are true, that the Earth will once again be pure and green, the animals flourish, and the waters run clean. When these things come to be, we Lenapé have been told that we will then have our lands back.

There is much that is wrong in the land, much that should not be here. And so it is, we eastern Lenapé are as strangers in our land, surrounded by a culture directly at odds with our philosophy, our spirituality and traditions. So, for now, we must live in two worlds, with one foot in and one foot out, and the trick is learning to balance the two without falling flat on our faces. This we have had to learn to survive and to keep the ways of our ancestors alive.

THE PEOPLE

Our Lenapé people, Lenape'wàk as we call ourselves, were called "the Grandfathers" and considered the progenitors of all the Algonquin peoples. Lenapé means "common people."

All of the Algonquin peoples speak similar languages. Among these peoples are:

INTRODUCTION

Ottawa
Ojibwe (Chippewa)
Sauk
Fox
Menomini
Miami
Piankeshaw*
Potawatomi
Kickapoo
Illinois*

Powhatan*
Canoy*
Nanticoke
Mahican
Mohegan
Cree
Cheyenne
Blackfoot
Lenapé (Delaware)
Shawnee

New England Tribes:
Wappinger*
Abnaki
Penobscot
Massachuset*
Wampanoag
Pequot*
Narranganset
Micmac
Maliseet

Long Island Tribes: out of about one dozen or so principal
tribes here, only these exist today:
Shinnecock
Montauk
Poosepatuck
*Extinct tribes

Our Lenapé people are also called the Delaware, but we don't refer to ourselves by this name. "Delaware" is derived from the third Lord de la Warr, Sir Thomas West, who was governor of the English colony of Jamestown, Virginia in 1610. One of his captains, Samuel Argall, went up the Atlantic coast to seek provisions for the Virginia colonists and on his way back he sailed into the bay of the Delaware River, and he named it in honor of Governor de la Warr (who never saw it in his lifetime). After a while, the Native peoples living along the river, which emptied into the bay, became known as Delaware Indians.

There were three main divisions of our Lenapé people, the Munsee, Unami, and the Unalaxtako (or Jersey), each living in a different area, and each speaking slightly different dialects of a similar language.

The Munsee (Minsi, or Minisink), who were often called "the Wolves," or identified with the wolf, were the northernmost of the three. Their central council fire was at Minisink on the upper Delaware River. Their territory extended south from here to the Musconetcong Mountains (Muskanekàm) in northern New Jersey and the Lehigh River in Pennsylvania; west, to the

Susquehanna River; north, to the headwaters of the Delaware and Susquehanna Rivers and to the Catskill Mountains; and east, to the Hudson River.

The Unami, or "Down the River People," often identified with the turtle, lived below the Munsee lands, along both sides of the Delaware River and along the Lehigh and Schuylkill Rivers of Pennsylvania, and down into northern Delaware. The Delaware River was one of the sacred rivers of our Lenape'wàk, and we called it Lenapewihìtàk—River of the Lenapé. It was like the center, like the backbone of our peoples.

The Unalaxtako or Jersey people lived along the sea coast of New Jersey, and in the south of the state. They were often identified with the turkey.

Although there were three main divisions of our people, there also existed many of our relations nearby to us:

There were the Powhatans of the Chesapeake Bay-Potomac River regions of Maryland and Virginia;

The Nanticokes, from Delaware, Maryland and up to the Potomac River. We called them Unextako;

The Mohegans of Connecticut, and numerous Algonquin speaking tribes throughout New England;

The Mahikani (erroneously called Mohicans), who lived along the banks of the Hudson River. They were also given a wolf apellation;

The Montauk, Shinnecock, Patchogues, and other tribes of Long Island.

Then there were the Shawnee, "People from the South," who long ago left Lenape'hokink and went south, staying near the Creeks. Then, in the eighteenth century they came back north and interspersed among us, many going to settle in Ohio. In the east they are said to have settled in with the Mahikani. They also settled between the forks of the Delaware and to where the Schuylkill meets the Delaware River.

The origins of the Native American peoples are often thought to have begun with Asiatic peoples who crossed the Bering land bridge in the remote past, to Alaska and thus into North America. However, many Native Americans hold an opposite view, that our people traveled from here to Siberia. The truth of the matter

INTRODUCTION

is that it was probably a little of both, since there exist both similarities and differences between our Native American people and the native peoples of Siberia. The Hopi elders tell of migrations long ago to the north door (Alaska) from the four corners area of the U.S. Archaeological evidence shows older dates for North American than Siberian sites and finds, seemingly supporting the Hopi elders' view. However, the Eskimos and the northwest coast tribes among others have strong Asiatic features. Then there is the matter of blood types. Eskimo and Mongolian people have type B blood, whereas most Native American people are type O. So, there is evidence that migration happened in both directions, and I believe that is exactly what occurred.

According to our Lenapé traditions, we had our origins in the cold north (in Canada, I believe). It was said that after a great flood, the climate changed and it became very cold. So, coming together in Council, the people decided to search out warmer lands to the south, and so our prophets guided us from their visions and were led by Spirit to our present lands which we call Lenape'hokink.

From out of the cold northern lands we came, many thousands of our people. Our journey was long, and we stayed for lengths of time at different places along the way. Some of our people remained at these places, but most kept going.

Finally, our Lenape'wàk reached Namès Sipu (the Fish River)—the Mississippi River—and followed it down, until coming close to where the Allegewi Sipu (Ohio River) empties into the Mississippi. Here we camped while our warriors scouted the country across the river, to the east. While camped here we came into contact with the Menkwe (Iroquois), who had also migrated from distant lands, and had come upon this river further up near its source. The Menkwe were of the same purpose as our Lenape'wàk, they were proceeding to the east until they found a country that they found suitable. Our scouts discovered that the country east of the Namès Sipu was inhabited by a very powerful Nation, who had many large towns built on the great rivers flowing through their land. These people called themselves Tallegewi (Tàlekewi—probably the Cherokee, who call

7

themselves Tsalagi). They were said to be remarkably tall, and there were giants among them, people much taller than the tallest Lenapé.

When the Lenapé arrived on the banks of Namès Sipu, they sent to the Tallegewi to request permission to cross their country in search of uninhabited country towards the rising sun, where our prophets directed us. This they agreed to, and our Lenape'wàk had begun to cross Namés Sipu, when the Tallegewi, seeing the great numbers of our people, grew treacherous. When half of our people were across the great river, they fell upon us, cutting off our retreat and preventing the rest of our people from coming across to our aid, threatening them with destruction. Angered at the great loss of warriors due to the treachery of the Tallegewi and not being properly prepared for war, our chiefs councilled together as to what to do. Were they to retreat or to try their strength? They chose to fight, and they sent word to the Menkwe, to ask for their help. The Menkwe readily agreed to join us in the conflict, and it was decided that if we should overcome the Tallegewi together, that we would divide their country between us. The Menkwe proposal was accepted and our two Nations resolved to conquer or die.

Having thus united their warriors, we both declared war against the Tallegewi. Great battles were fought, and many warriors fell on both sides. The Tallegewi fortified their large towns and erected defenses, especially on large rivers, and near lakes, where they were repeatedly attacked and stormed by our combined forces. One battle took place in which hundreds fell, who were afterwards buried together in heaps and covered over with earth. The Tallegewi, at last, realized their destruction was inevitable if they did not flee, and they abandoned their country to us. They fled down the Namès Sipu, from whence they never returned. So we divided these lands, the Menkwe choosing that part north, near the Great Lakes and their tributary streams, and the Lenapé taking possession of the country to the south of that.

So, our Lenapé people settled that country and lived there for many years; but our hunters discovered more land east of the mountains which was uninhabited. So many of our people proceeded towards the rising sun. They went down the Great Bay River (Susquehanna River) and then into Chesapeake Bay itself. As they traveled, by land and water, sometimes near the great Saltwater Lake, the Atlantic Ocean, they discovered the Great River, which is now called the Delaware, which we call Lenapewihìtàk. Exploring still further eastward, into what is now New Jersey, they then arrived at another great river, the Hudson, called by us, Mahikanìtàk. These were clearly the lands to which our prophets had led us—untouched, pure and pristine, with an abundance of fish and game. Our people at last settled on four great rivers—the Delaware, Hudson, Susquehanna, and the Potomac. The Delaware River, Lenapewihìtàk, was made the center of our Nation.

However, the whole of our people did not reach this country. Many remained behind, not crossing the Namès Sipu. They had retreated into the lands on the west side after seeing the hostile reception that those who crossed had received from the Tallegewi.

Thus our people finally became divided into three separate bodies: one half settled along the Atlantic Ocean to the east; some to the west, beyond Namès Sipu; and others along the east side of Namès Sipu. In the lands near the Atlantic were the Lenapé, Mahikani and the New England tribes; on the west of the Mississippi were such peoples as the Cheyenne, Arapaho, and Blackfeet; and on the east of the Mississippi such peoples as the Sauk, Fox, Potawatami, and Kickapoo. All of these Algonquin peoples were originally one people in the past, we Lenapé, remembered as such to this day, and called the Grandfathers.

For many thousands of years in our lands of Lenape'hokink, our people and their Algonquin grandchildren lived close to the land. We lived in harmony, and did not despoil the Earth or the living things around us. Our world was pristine, of unparalleled beauty and purity. What we had need of the land gave us. We took only the plant and animal life that we needed and left some for others and for the future generations, or to go to seed and to reproduce.

We didn't cut down live trees to any great extent, but used dead wood for our fires. Trees are great spiritual entities, so we believe, and their spirits give power to and sustain the spirit of a particular area. To cut down great numbers of trees is to weaken and damage the land around us, and can only bring eventual harm to ourselves.

For food we hunted animals and birds and caught fish. Bear, moose, elk, deer, beaver, etc. were among those animals hunted, as were grouse, turkeys, geese and duck. Fish were caught using lines and bone hooks, speared or caught in weirs and nets. Ocean-run shad were a great food staple along the rivers going to the ocean, as were oysters, clams, etc. among those of our people living on the coast. Each family had its own hunting territory, and several families might hunt a particular area one year and hunt in another area the next, giving the other areas a rest, so that they wouldn't deplete the animals.

Before setting out to hunt, the hunters would burn tobacco, giving prayers to Misinkhâlikàn, the Forest Guardian and Keeper of the Game Animals, to insure their success, that their food needs would be met. Offering tobacco was the way given to us to communicate with our Creator and the spirits. It was like food or money to the spirits; the smell of burning tobacco greatly pleases them, and the smoke carries our thoughts and prayers to them that we might be heard.

When an animal was killed, it was thought that the animal gave itself to us, and we gave thanks to it, and offered tobacco to its spirit. Everything that could be used from an animal was put to use, nothing was wasted. The skins were made into bedding and clothing, the meat was eaten or dried for later use, the bones were made into tools, needles or ornaments, etc. When a young hunter killed his first deer, it was the custom to give it to an older person who lived alone or to someone in need, as a lesson in generosity.

We held the eating of certain animals to be *kula'kàn* or taboo. These included rabbit, woodchuck, rattlesnake, horse, dog, wildcat, panther, fox, wolf and muskrat.

For hunting, we used spears, bolas, and bows and arrows. Our knives were made of flint, as were the points of our arrows and spears. In fact, flint is sharper than the finest steel, and so a flint knife is not perhaps as primitive or inferior as one might think.

INTRODUCTION

Our Lenape'wàk ancestors grew much of their own food, as well as foraging for fruits, wild greens, nuts and roots. The principal crops grown were corn, beans, pumpkins, squash and tobacco. Melons were also grown, but whether these were in fact introduced by the Europeans is a subject of debate.

Corn, *xaskwim*, was one of our main food staples. Fresh corn was roasted on hot coals, leaving the husks on while cooking. White corn, *pawim*, was soaked in water with wood ashes added to remove the hulls, and making the corn swell to make hominy. Blue corn, *sèsapsink*, was dried, roasted and made into a fine meal which was used as a high energy and filling staple for hunters and warriors. Blue corn thus prepared was called *tèsamana'ne*. Corn was also mixed with beans to make what we know today as succotash. Dried corn was sometimes cooked and eaten, but was usually pounded into cornmeal in a mortar made of a hollowed section of hardwood log, using a wooden or stone pestle. Cornmeal was used to make *sa'panmush*, or dumplings. Bread was made from cornmeal mixed with water and formed into small patties and baked on a hot stone.

Ears of corn were braided together by their husks and hung from the rafters of the house. Stored this way, they were called *xapânkwe*. Beans were dried and corn kernels removed and stored in bark containers or baskets. Pumpkins and squash were cut into rings and dried. Fish and meat was smoked and dried to preserve it.

After the white people, Wapsitàk, started trading furs for other goods with us—steel knives, kettles, tools, etc.—we soon forgot the old ways of napping flint to make knives, steel tools replaced what we used to make of stone, pottery making was forgotten, etc. We forgot our old technologies and, through the fur trade, became dependent on European goods. It wasn't long before the population of beavers and fur-bearing animals began to plummet, and they became very scarce. Soon we had only the land itself to use to purchase those things we were now dependent upon to survive, and we lost much land through this process.

Before the coming of the white people, we Lenapé knew no intoxicating substances. We had no alcoholic drink, narcotics or hallucinogens. These weren't part of our culture. With the coming of alcohol, many problems came to our people, often resulting in the loss of our lands. Our prophets and holy men urged the people to keep from it as it was ruining our way of life, creating much trouble, fighting and discord. But many did not listen or became dependent on it.

Tobacco was held to be sacred to us and was not abused. Nor was it a vice to our people as it is in modern culture. First, tobacco, or *ksha'te*, was not inhaled to any great extent and it was not grown with dangerous chemical fertilizers as is today's product. Also, our Native tobacco is a different kind from that used in modern tobacco products. Tobacco as found today in cigars, cigarettes, pipe and chewing tobacco comes from *Nicotiana tobaccum*, originally native to the Caribbean. Our Native tobacco is *Nicotiana rustica*, and is much stronger and more potent than *Nicotiana tobaccum*. Usually we mixed herbs and barks with tobacco, and different tribes had their own mixes of these that they used. Common mixing ingredients used were: bearberry leaves, red osier dogwood bark, spruce needles, sumach leaves, etc. Tobacco, being sacred, was used to offer smoke in prayer, sending our thoughts to the Creator and spirits. Tobacco was seen as conducive to thinking, and was often smoked when contemplating a problem or situation. It also attracted the spirits to what one was doing and thus it was hoped they would give their blessings to whatever was being undertaken. When a visitor came, they were first offered tobacco and a pipe. Any time people came together in Council, the men would first smoke their pipes, the smoke joining together into one smoke, and their minds into one mind. Any time we killed an animal, picked herbs or plants, planted or harvested crops, before we ate, gave thanksgiving, gave prayer, crossed a stream or started a trip by canoe, tobacco was burned or offered. Our way of life was based on regular thanksgiving for what we received, and tobacco was the medium for this, our offering to the spirits for their blessings and aid.

Our people usually lived in small villages, comprising a small number of families. These were mostly situated on rivers or streams, as one of our main methods of travel was by canoe.

12

Such a location also gave us easy access for fishing, and provided a quick means of escape if we were attacked by our enemies. Foot trails ran from one village to another. These Indian paths, as they are popularly known, were about eighteen inches wide, and provided easy crossing of rivers and enabled travelers to go over mountains and forests without getting lost. Paths were given names according to where they ended. Many modern roads follow near our old paths, which the early white settlers turned into wagon roads and which eventually gave way to modern highways.

Family was and is very important to our people. Extended families of grandparents, and sometimes uncles and aunts, lived together in the larger *wikwama* (houses). Some of these were as much as sixty feet long and twenty feet wide. *Wikwama* were of three types: round with a dome-shaped roof; rectangular with an arched roof; or rectangular with a ridge pole and a pitched roof. They were built of a bent sapling frame, with crossties, tied together where they joined. The outside was covered with sheets of bark stripped from chestnut, elm, or basswood trees. There were no windows, the door was a hide, located away from the prevailing wind and it was the only opening except for a hole or two in the roof over the inside firepit. Food was stored in a pit in the ground, either inside or outside. Cooking was done on an inside or outside fire, food being cooked in pointed-bottom clay pots held upright in the fire by supporting stones. Tiered platforms of skin-covered poles were built along the walls and served as seats or beds.

In Lenapé society, relationship and inheritance is determined through the women. When a Chief died, the position would go to his sister's oldest son. Children belong to the clan of their mother. People of the same clan, even if separated by great distances, and not of immediate family relation, are considered relatives, both by blood and by spirit. According to our traditions, one of our taboos or restrictions, *kulaka'na*, is that one cannot marry another of their clan. To do so is viewed as incestuous.

We Lenapé have three clans (*lake'in*): Pele, the Turkey clan; Poko'unko, the Turtle clan; and Tuksit, the Wolf clan.

Marriages were not attended with vows or ceremony. Marriage

13

among our Lenape'wàk was not understood as being a life-long commitment. It was our custom that a man and woman live together only as long as they were pleased with each other. Either could divorce the other as they pleased. However, marriage was considered a serious undertaking, and was not just jumped into. Couples usually stayed together their whole lives, especially if they had children, and adultery was a rare occurrence. A man had to be a good hunter and show the woman's family that he could provide for her. A period of courting was first undertaken: a man would let a woman know he was interested in her by courting her with a flute, composing a song just for her. If she was also interested, she would meet with the man, he would ask her if she would be his wife, and if she agreed, and was pleased with him, the man would give gifts and ask for the parents' agreement through another man, usually a relative, who acted as a go-between. When all was satisfactory, the man and woman would go off together, build a *wikwàm*, and were considered to be married.

There has been much written in the past about the status of Native women, and many people still have the mistaken view that our Native women were treated as slaves. Nothing could be further from the truth. We Lenapé have always held women and men to be equal. One was not seen as superior to the other, and the work was divided between each, and was somewhat harder for the men. It was the women's part to keep their family alive and whole. There were things that were done by women and there were things that were done by men, each knowing what was expected of them and each knowing their place in the life of the village. Women owned the house, and the children were considered hers should divorce occur. Women took care of the children, cooked the food, prepared hides and made clothes, planted seeds, tended the garden, harvested the crops, cut and gathered firewood, and ground corn in a mortar. Men built the houses and repaired them, made axes, hoes, dishes, bowls, and other household necessities and tools, made canoes out of hollowed logs, protected the village from enemies, and hunted. Hunting was done all year round, and provided the household with meat for food and skins for clothing. Every day

14

at daybreak the men would go off to hunt and would return in mid-morning with game. In the winter the men also trapped. Upon the man's exertions as a hunter and the woman's work taking care of the home and crops, did the survival of our people depend.

Women gave birth standing up, which made for an easier delivery, and the mother was attended to by other women in a special lodge or a special woman's room in the *wikwàm*. Men weren't allowed to come near them at this time. Babies were tied to a cradleboard, and this was fastened to a woman's back. In the cradleboard, the baby was always close to its mother, giving it a great sense of security and closeness. On the cradleboard the baby went everywhere that its mother went and a strong and close bond developed between mother and child. At night the cradleboard served as a crib. When the baby outgrew the cradleboard, it was taught to walk. Babies were never left alone as there was always someone in the family to care for them. When five or six years old, children started to learn the ways of either the men, playing in imitation of their fathers, or the women, helping their mothers in their daily duties. Children were rarely punished physically, and were generally well behaved.

In appearance, our people were striking to the early Europeans. With long black hair, swarthy to near black skin, high prominent cheekbones and painted faces, sometimes with tattoos, our people were comely and handsome. Our people were often taller than the white men. We kept ourselves very clean and were very neat in dress and appearance.

Clothing was made of skins, feathers and plant material, sewn and held together with thread made from sinew. Women wore dresses, men shirts, and both wore leggings, all being made from deerskin. Moccasins were also made of deerskin, and decorated with shell beads, porcupine quills, bells, etc. Men wore a loin cloth or breech clout of soft buckskin, which passed between the legs and was brought up and folded over a deerskin belt, front and back. An interesting cross-cultural exchange took place after a while between the Native and white peoples: where our Native people first dressed in deerskin clothing, after the introduction of cloth in trading we started to wear cloth clothing and European-style clothing, and the whites took up our deerskin clothing with the fringe.

Men and women wore stone and shell pendants, beads, necklaces, armbands and anklets, and earrings of stone, shells, animal teeth and claws.

In wintertime fur robes and leggings were worn; women sometimes wore shawls of feathers.

Hair was worn long by both men and women. It was looked upon as a thing sacred and unique to each person, a kind of signature, placed by the Creator upon each person at birth. It was one's connection to spirit. Older men let their hair grow long, down beyond the shoulders. Boys and young men shaved their heads with a sharp flint, leaving a crest of long hair in the center which was greased to make it stand erect, or a long length of hair on a shaved head called a scalp lock was worn and decorated with shells, etc. according to personal preference.

Beards were not usually worn, the hairs being regularly pulled out using mussel shells as tweezers. However, face hair grew back and became finer the more it was pulled. Men pulled out their facial hairs when they wished to paint their faces for war or ceremony. By 1800, most of the men could be found having scant, wispy beards.

Both men and women painted their faces using various colors according to personal design, and men often painted their bodies as well. Women commonly used red, making a spot on their cheeks, and painting the ears or around the eyes.

Tattooing was also widely practiced by men and women. A design was drawn and pricked along the outline with a needle until blood was drawn, and then, burnt, powdered poplar tree bark was spread thereon.

Thus were the lifeways of my ancestors. However, as every life must one day come to an end in death, we have many traditions concerning it. In our view of life, we believe in a soul that survives death. We call the soul or spirit, *lenapeâkàn*. When the heart stops, the soul has separated from the body and then we hold a person to be dead. At death, we believe that the spirit departs from the body but remains nearby.

INTRODUCTION

We also believe that the blood itself is a soul, and separate from the main soul or spirit. This blood soul we believe we are to take with the body into the ground and so embalming is discouraged.

When a person dies, we open a door or window a crack to allow the spirit of the deceased to travel as it wishes and sees fit, to make its preparations before passing on.

Upon a death, the women of the family would pound dried hominy in a mortar and a bread was made from this for the funeral feast, called *lenapâna*. No salt was put into this, or in any of the food for the feast.

An all-night vigil, or wake, was held by those who came to view the body. This started at sundown, and at midnight prayers were said for the deceased, the family and relatives. After this ceremony a feast was given. To keep awake we used to play what we call *chipakwinalitìn*, the moccasin game, our Native version of the pea and shell game. This game was played among many Native tribes in North America.

The face of the deceased was painted with *olàmàn* (a sacred red paint), so that when they stood before the Creator, they would be recognized as Lenapé. For a woman, a spot was put on each cheek and in the parting of the hair, and for a man three small lines were painted from the outside of the eyes back towards the hairline.

Burials were done as soon as possible and before noon, and the head of the deceased was pointed to the east. No coffins were used prior to the arrival of the white man. The corpse was placed instead on a bark and moss mat and covered with bark, fully dressed. Belongings of the dead were buried with them. When coffins did come into use, a hole was cut in it to allow the spirit to get out.

A grave marker, *kinkinhikàn*, was placed at the head of the grave as the grave was filled in. Then it was painted with *olàmàn*. This grave marker was made of wood and was not replaced; it was left to rot back into the ground. For a man the marker was a straight board with a diamond cut at the top; for a woman, a cross with diamonds at the top and ends.

It was our belief that some people should not be present at

17

funerals: a person who was sick, as it was thought to weaken them further; a person who was disliked by the deceased; pregnant women and children. The spirits of the dead might harm such people.

A funeral feast, called *takwiphâtin*, was held at the head of the grave. Only virtuous women could prepare food for such a feast, and a menstruating woman was never allowed to touch it.

Before everyone left, a small fire was made at the head of the grave, and was rekindled for the next three evenings just before sundown. This fire was made so that the deceased could take the fire with them to the spirit world to keep warm on their journey.

A year of mourning was observed. If a woman had lost her husband, a relative of the husband would take her hair down, and it was left loose for one year. Married women usually wore their hair tied into a bun on the back of the head. She would have no social contact in this time and she blackened her face, as a sign of mourning.

After a year had passed, the spouse of the deceased was smudged with cedar smoke and prayed for, and then they could begin to socialize once more. The relatives of the dead person would give the surviving spouse new clothes, thought of as a new skin, and this person was then free to remarry. Often a *wihunge*, or annual memorial feast was given for the deceased at this time.

THE LENAPÉ ENCOUNTER WITH EUROPEANS

Our Lenapé people have always been a generous people, and so we were when the Dutch first reached our lands in the early 1600s. We gave them land, taught them how to grow corn and showed them our utmost hospitality; but they were treacherous in their dealings with us. The little land we gave them wasn't enough, and they wanted more and more, finally resorting to much warfare with our people, and pushing us further away from our ancient homelands near the New York City area.

Next came the Swedes, but we didn't have too many problems with these people. However, the Dutch eventually took over their settlements along the Delaware River.

Then came the English, who usurped the Dutch. We called them Jenkise, from which comes the modern word Yankee. They took over all of the lands of the Dutch and then they started a long, slow process of removing us from our lands with much resulting warfare.

The English claimed that all of the land in America belonged to the British Crown by right of discovery. They recognized the right of our Indian people to occupy the land, until relinquished by deed, treaty or conquest, but did not consider our people to be true owners of the land.

Our people did not understand the European concept of buying or selling land. Land to us was like the air, sunlight and water, something that was necessary for our survival, for our very lives. Our thought was that we were giving the whites some land to live on for a while. We saw it as sharing with them, and did not consider giving them the use of the land permanently. We certainly had no intention of excluding ourselves from using it. However, when our Chiefs signed deeds and treaties, to the European mind it meant a permanent transfer of ownership. In giving the whites land, we were being hospitable, as was our custom. The payments in goods that we received were not seen as payment, but as gifts of generosity from the whites, for permitting them to share the use of the land with us. Thus, we did not fully understand the view of the whites when giving deeds for land, and when we did realize that we had dispossessed ourselves, it was too late to do anything about it. There was also much deception in persuading our people to sacrifice our rights of occupancy. White buyers would get our Chiefs drunk and then take advantage of them in land dealings, to sign away our rights to the land.

So, the English did give us much trouble, until William Penn, whom we called our good brother Miquon (*mikwân* = quill), came to our lands in what is now called Pennsylvania. A great friendship formed between him and our Lenapé people. The Iroquois called him Onas, and we eventually adopted this name for him. Brother Onas became an expression used by our people after Penn's death in referring to the Pennsylvania government.

Penn/Miquon negotiated a peace treaty with our Lenapé people at Shackamaxon under a great elm tree, following his arrival in Philadelphia in the fall of 1652. Although there is no documentary evidence of this treaty, in the Museum of the American Indian in New York City there exist the wampum belts we gave to William Penn, called the Penn Treaty Belts, at the Treaty of Shackamaxon in 1683.

(Wampum belts were belts made of cylindrical beads, made from conch shells and the quahaug clam. These belts, often having designs of purple and white wampum beads, were used to seal treaties and agreements between the Native tribes and the Americans, English and French, etc., or between different Native tribes. Such agreements and treaties made with wampum can be compared with oaths sworn on the Bible, being sacred and ever-binding statements made before the Creator, and not to be broken or taken lightly.)

William Penn was Governor of Pennsylvania in the late 1600s and he made several purchases of lands from us. It was never his intention to force us from our homes on the lands he purchased. Miquon/Onas held that white people and the Indian could live together in harmony, and that we should be treated as equals. During his lifetime we had no complaints over land matters that were not able to be resolved to our satisfaction. However, upon his death others came into power who were not friendly towards us, and who were greedy for our lands.

In 1737, after much argument, threats and pressure from James Logan, head of Indian Affairs, the Walking Purchase was signed by our Chiefs, Nutimus, Tishecunk, Lappawinso, and Menakihikon. Through this we lost most of our lands in eastern Pennsylvania. By bringing forth a fake 1686 deed supposedly signed by some of our former Chiefs, Logan insisted that boundaries had never been laid out, and so we agreed that the English could have as much land as a man could walk in a day and a half. But Logan came up with a devious plan. He had paths cut through the woods in advance and used three specially trained fast walkers who were followed by horses with provisions. So the end result was that instead of covering 25 miles as expected, 60 miles was taken in. But this wasn't the end of the deception. By manipulation on paper, more land was marked, and it included all of the lands occupied by our people and some Shawnee.

This gave rise to a lot of resentment among our people. We felt frustrated and tricked, so we refused to move, and threatened all intruders into our lands. The English moved settlers in, and this made us even more angry and several incidents of violence erupted. Now, as a thorn in the side of the English, they wished to be rid of us. So, Brother Onas (the Pennsylvania government) showed the Six Nations Iroquois Confederacy Chiefs the fake 1686 deed and they stood against us and forbade us to sell any land. We were caught between the English and the Six Nations, and so had no choice but to move our people from our lands at the forks of the Delaware to the Susquehanna River. Also adding to our anger was white encroachment on our lands on the Brandywine River and the forcing of our people from that area also.

In the switch from William Penn's humanitarian policies to Logan's divide-and-rule policy of strengthening our uncles, the Six Nations, our Chiefs felt helpless and frustrated, victims of an injustice against which we could do nothing. The favoritism shown to the Six Nations was highly resented by us. We were innocent victims of an Indian policy that served the best interests of the English in their resistance to the French, a policy that strengthened the Six Nations but left our Lenapé people without a country to call our own.

In 1742, the last band of our people was forced to move from the junction of the Lehigh and Delaware Rivers to the Susquehanna. The Susquehanna Valley was claimed by the Cayugas and Oneidas of the Six Nations, who were allies of the English. It was with the consent of our Cayuga and Oneida uncles that we were allowed to settle on the Susquehanna.

Being scattered in several villages and with many different Chiefs, it was difficult for the Pennsylvania government to conduct negotiations with us as a people. So, Brother Onas felt that if there were one King or Leader over all of our Lenapé people, that it would be easier in this respect. So, they looked

21

for just the right man, one who could be bribed, easily influenced and intimidated. They found their puppet in Chief Sassoonan (Sàsunan), an elderly man who was easily controlled, addicted to rum and who lacked moral fortitude.

Pennsylvania's new Indian policy was set up to give the Six Nations complete control over any Indians who retreated to the Susquehanna. Many migrant tribes fell under their domination: the Shawnee, Nanticoke, Twightwee (Miami), Mahican, Conoy, Conestoga, and Tutelo, driven from their Native homelands by pressures from the English settlers.

After Sassoonan's death, the Pennsylvania government decided to allow the Six Nations to select the Delaware King/Leader. This allowed them to exert even more control over us. In 1752, the Iroquois chose Shingas as our Principal Chief.

In 1754, the French and Indian War broke out, and the Six Nations decided to lend their support to the English. To the surprise of the Six Nations, Shingas, who they thought they had under their thumb, took sides with the French, and from Ohio, he and the Shawnee launched attacks on the Pennsylvania, Maryland, and Virginia frontiers.

In the meantime, our people on the Susquehanna found a leader in Teedyuskung. At first he was neutral, but finally he too sided with the French in 1755. Teedyuskung directed war parties, spreading fear and terror across the frontier in eastern Pennsylvania, southern New York and New Jersey.

The Walking Purchase was still fresh in our minds, and though we had no love for the French, we held a deep animosity towards the English, due to their deceit, broken promises and intrusion, and our expulsion from our homelands, together with the spreading of smallpox and the sale of alcohol among our people. From our point of view, the deaths of friends and relatives were due to evils brought by the English, who had confiscated our lands in the Delaware River Valley. We believed that they were trying to destroy our people.

In 1756, Governor Robert Morris of Pennsylvania declared war on my Lenapé people, offering cash bounties for captives or scalps. A year later, Governor Jonathan Belcher of New Jersey issued a proclamation declaring our people enemies, rebels and traitors. He too offered cash bounties for our scalps or for any of our people taken captive.

Pennsylvania's Indian policy fell apart when our people and the Shawnee went on the warpath. We turned a deaf ear to our Iroquois uncles.

The headquarters of our Chiefs, Shingas and Captain Jacobs, was a large town called Kittanning, near present-day Kittanning, Pennsylvania, and from here they planned their attacks upon the frontier. In 1756, some three hundred British soldiers attacked this town and burnt it to the ground, killing Captain Jacobs, among others, and destroying our provisions supplied by the French. Of one hundred white prisoners held by our people, only a few were rescued, as we took them with us. Many of our so-called white "captives" remained with us by their own choice. The majority of captives were adopted and treated by us as members of our tribe and families. Very few prisoners were ever tortured or killed. White captives often found our way of life more to their liking than their own society.

With Kittanning destroyed, our people under Shingas moved to Shenango (near Sharon, Pennsylvania), Saukunk (Beaver, Pennsylvania), and Kuskusky (New Castle, Pennsylvania), which became one of our largest settlements. These villages were hard for the English to reach, and the French were between us and the English, at Fort Duquesne.

In 1758, the British attacked Fort Duquesne and set it afire. The French fled and here the English built Fort Pitt, in what is now Pittsburgh, Pennsylvania.

Shingas' brother, Beaver, took over as Chief of our people on the Ohio. In 1759, while he was arranging peace with the English at Fort Pitt, Teedyuskung was negotiating for peace for our people on the Susquehanna, at Easton, Pennsylvania. All of our people were now nominally at peace with the English, but it was more of an uneasy truce than a lasting peace.

Our people under Teedyuskung, on the Susquehanna, were given a place to settle, at Wyoming, Pennsylvania. However, it was not long before Connecticut settlers appeared, causing us more anxiety. Beaver sent a message to Teedyuskung and Nutimus at Tioga (Athens, Pa.) to come west and join him in the Ohio country, but even though the Chiefs considered this, the Pennsylvania government did not favor it and talked them out of it. They were hoping that our people would deter the Connecticut settlers from establishing themselves in Pennsylvania.

More and more Connecticut people began to trespass on our land and in April of 1763, our Chief, Teedyuskung, was killed when his house was set on fire along with the other houses at Wyoming. The next morning our village lay in ashes, so we fled, some to Moravian missions and others to the Big Island (Lock Haven, Pa.) where there were others of our people. Still others moved to the Tuscarawas in Ohio, or north, joining the Iroquois on the Grand River in Ontario, Canada, where their descendants live to this day.

(The Moravians were German missionaries who brought Christianity to our Lenapé and other Native peoples in Pennsylvania and Ohio. The Moravian converts, or Christian Indians, were forbidden to engage in acts of violence, even the defense of their lands. The Moravians looked down upon our Lenapé lifeways and spirituality, and were greatly responsible for a loss of culture and lands among my people. They weakened the Native people and our resistance to the whites who encroached on our lands. The Christian Indians, being pacifists, often became sitting ducks for white people seeking revenge for acts committed against them by other Native peoples.)

One condition on which Beaver had been willing to settle for peace was that whites would not be permitted to settle west of the Alleghenny Mountains. When the English drove the French out of Ohio, they started to make their occupation permanent. Christian Post, a Moravian missionary who negotiated peace between our Lenapé and the English, and George Croghan, Deputy Indian agent for the Crown, gave our people assurances that as soon as the French were driven away, the English would withdraw and no settlers would be permitted west of the Alleghennies. However, plans were already being made for settlers to move in.

We were completely dependent upon trade for powder and lead for hunting and for our necessities. Severe restrictions on items for our survival were implemented by the Governor General of British North America, Lord Jeffrey Amherst. These restrictions, and the consistent failure of the English to keep their promises, were the main reasons we joined in Pontiac's War in 1763.

Pontiac's War was a Native effort to unite the tribes to resist the westward expansion and invasion of our lands by the English. It has often been called a conspiracy, but was actually a series of uprisings started when the Seneca sent wampum war belts to the Ohio tribes in 1761 and 1763, urging our Lenapé people and others to join with them against the English, who were said to be deliberately withholding powder from us to weaken us, and were bent on destroying us all. This, added to a decrease in gifts given to our peoples, a prohibition on the sale of liquor, and English deceit in not leaving Ohio after the defeat of the French, incited Pontiac, an Ottawa Chief, into action. He was also greatly influenced by a medicine man of our Lenapé people, who told the Indians to go back to their old ways, making things using our old technologies instead of purchasing trade goods, and to drive the whites from our lands.

After the destruction of most of the smaller forts on the Alleghenny River, our Lenapé, the Shawnee, Mingo and other Indian warriors from Ohio layed siege to Fort Pitt. Two of our Lenapé, Turtle's Heart and Mamaltee, visited Captain Simeon Ecuyer at Fort Pitt, to tell him that the other Alleghenny forts had fallen, and to advise him to give up Fort Pitt before the Indians overran it and put all the occupants to death. He thanked them for their warning and in appreciation he gave them two blankets and a handkerchief as presents, which were in fact taken from the beds of smallpox patients.

Many of the Native people believed that the white man was purposefully trying to destroy them, and indeed there is much evidence to back up their assertion. Lord General Jeffrey Amherst, the English Governor General of North America, wrote the following in a letter to Col. Henry Bouquet: "Could it not be contrived to send the smallpox among the disaffected tribes of Indians? We must on this occasion use every stratagem in our power to reduce them." Col. Bouquet replied that he would try to spread an epidemic by giving the Indians blankets infected with smallpox. Lord Amherst said in return, "You will do well to try to inoculate the Indians by means of blankets, as well as to try every other method that can serve to extirpate this execrable race." It was after receipt of this letter that Turtle's Heart and Mamaltee were given the infected blankets.

When Ecuyer refused to vacate Fort Pitt, our warriors attacked settlements in the Juniata, Tuscarora, and Cumberland valleys. In the meantime, Captain Bull, son of Teedyuskung, was sending war parties throughout the Wyoming valley in eastern Pennsylvania.

Col. Henry Bouquet broke the siege of Fort Pitt in the same year (1763) and our Lenapé and Shawnee warriors retreated back to the Ohio country.

In December of the same year, a group of vigilantes called the Paxton Boys engaged in two massacres of the unarmed Christian Conestoga Indians living in Lancaster, Pennsylvania, killing, scalping and hacking limbs from defenseless men, women, and children. They then threatened to kill 140 Moravian (Christian) Lenapé, but Governor John Penn sent our people to Philadelphia for safety. However, due to threats from the citizenry they were sent north to Albany, and eventually they were sent back and kept under armed guard at Philadelphia for about a year, where they lost many people to smallpox and other diseases. Their survivors settled at Wyalusing.

In the summer of 1764, there were more raids, scalpings and attacks on the settlements. Col. John Armstrong, who had previously destroyed Kittanning, destroyed the Indian settlements at Big Island. The Indians retaliated by again attacking white settlements in the Wyoming valley. Under public pressure, Governor John Penn reinstated bounties for the scalps of enemy Indians.

Finally, late in 1764, Col. Bouquet subdued our Lenapé, Shawnee, Mingo, and Mahican peoples in Ohio. Peace talks ensued, and one of the terms was the return of all captives. Two hundred white captives were thus returned, but Bouquet had to station armed guards over them to prevent them from returning to their Indian homes.

While Col. Bouquet was marching against our people in Ohio, Sir William Johnson, Head of Indian Affairs of the Northern Colonies, sent a force to punish our people on the upper Susquehanna for our raids during Pontiac's War. In May of 1765 our people from both the Ohio and Susquehanna signed a peace treaty with Sir William. As punishment for our part in Pontiac's War, we lost all of our land rights until such time as the English and Six Nations decided where we were to live and hunt.

In 1768, the Six Nations signed the Treaty of Fort Stanwix, giving all of their lands south of the Susquehanna to Pennsylvania, and making the Ohio River the western limit of white territory. This treaty took from us our hunting grounds in Kentucky also.

In 1774, Koquethagecthon, "Captain White Eyes," became the leader of our people in Ohio. He was strongly pro-American, and when the Revolutionary War broke out between the English and the Americans, he refused to go to war and kept our people of Ohio neutral. However, our people in the upper Susquehanna and Chemung River valleys, along with the Wyandot (Huron), Chippewa (Ojibwe), Ottawa, Shawnee, Munsee and Mingoes joined with the English.

In 1778, at Fort Pitt, American politicians and military leaders met with three of our Chiefs from Ohio—Captain White Eyes, Captain John Killbuck, Sr., "Gelelemend," and Captain Pipe, also called Hopokàn and "Kogieschqwanoheel"—to sign a treaty. This was the first formal treaty between the U.S. government and an Indian tribe. It provided for an alliance between the Americans and our Lenapé people, and committed our warriors to helping the Americans.

The sixth article of this treaty stated that those Indians friendly to the U.S., with our Lenapé people at their head, would be permitted to form the 14th state in the American Union, and that they would have their own representatives in Congress. (However, whether the Americans were honest in giving our people hope of achieving equal status with the other thirteen states is questionable.)

Then, White Eyes was killed, but the circumstances surrounding his murder are not clear. Through his death the Americans lost a staunch supporter. Now, due to rumors spread by the English, Captain Pipe believed that the Americans were only pretending to be our friends in order to deceive us, and at the right time would seize our lands and destroy us. Captain Pipe believed

27

this was the secret policy of the Continental Congress and that it was his duty to organize our Lenapé people to prevent our destruction by the Americans.

Promises of the 1778 Treaty to us, for food, clothing, and gunpowder, were not fulfilled, and because of the failure of the Americans to assist our people, Killbuck, who was pro-American, lost prestige and influence among our people. So, with all support for the Americans gone from our leaders, Captain Pipe now jumped at this opportunity to persuade our Council to give support to the English, and we went on the warpath against the Americans.

General Daniel Brodhead received information at Fort Pitt from the Moravian missionaries that we were planning a surprise attack on the garrison. So he took 300 soldiers and marched to our principal town of Coshocton, in order to destroy it. He found only fifteen warriors there, and after trying them, his soldiers killed and scalped them. Old men, women and children were taken captive, and the town was burnt. The Christian Indians living in the surrounding Moravian mission towns were not molested by Brodhead's troops, after pleas from the missionaries.

In the meantime, the residents of Washington County in Pennsylvania had been subject to brutal Indian attacks, and they sought revenge against the Indians. So they organized a raiding party of 160 well-armed volunteers, seeking to avenge the assaults which they blamed on we Lenapé, and they set out to punish our people in Ohio. When they arrived in the Muskingum River country they found no warriors, our main town of Coshocton was in ashes and other towns had been deserted. The only Indians they found were the Christian Lenapé in the Moravian mission town of Gnadenhütten. Not being able to vent their frustrations, and seeking revenge, they accused our people there of giving aid and comfort to enemy Indians who had passed through their town. All of our people there were assembled, condemned for being accessories to murder and sentenced to death. On March 8, 1782, while they sang hymns, prayed and pleaded for mercy, they were all killed: 29 men, 27 women, and 34 children, 90 innocent victims in all. All of the dwellings were burnt, with all of the bodies put in one building for cremation.

When the news reached our main body of people it served to confirm Captain Pipe's suspicions, that the Americans were evil, bent on destroying our people. After this, our people lost all respect for the Americans. In addition, the efforts of the Christian missionaries began to lose their grip on our people. There was a great deal of mistrust.

In 1781, eleven months before the Gnadenhütten Massacre, one of our great Chiefs, Pachgantchihilas (Paxkanchihilas), better known as Buckongahelas, addressed our people in the mission town. His words were prophetic, as he unsuccessfully sought to persuade them to leave their exposed position on the Tuscarawas River to a place of safety among the Wyandots of the Maumee River.

He said, "I admit there are good white men, but they bear no proportion to the bad; the bad must be strongest, for they rule. They do what they please. They enslave those who are not of their color, although created by the same Great Spirit who created them. They would make slaves of us if they could, but as they cannot do it, they kill us! There is no faith to be placed in their words. They are not like the Indians, who are only enemies while at war, and are friends in peace. They will say to an Indian, 'My friend! My brother!' They will take him by the hand, and at the same moment, destroy him. And so you [addressing himself to the Christian Indians] will also be treated by them before long. Remember! that this day I have warned you to beware of such friends as these. I know the long knives [Americans], they are not to be trusted."

Buckongahelas died in 1805, but before he died he urged our people not to forsake our ancient customs nor trust the Americans lest we suffer the fate of the Indian converts at Gnadenhütten. He believed that in converting our people to Christianity, the whites were subtly weakening us before they chose to murder us.

In 1783, the British were defeated in the Revolutionary War. With our British allies no longer able to help us, thirty-five tribes, including our Lenapé people, met to form a confederacy to defend our lands.

Congress declared that the territory ceded to the U.S. by Britain in the Treaty of Paris was acquired by conquest, and that the U.S. had exclusive title to our Ohio lands.

In 1785, the Fort McIntosh Treaty was signed at what is now Beaver, Pennsylvania, with our Lenapé, Wyandot and some Chippewa and Ottawa. This allowed for white settlement in the Muskingum and Tuscarawas valleys. Many tribes and many Chiefs did not sign this treaty and were not represented in it. This treaty was greatly renounced, because the majority of Native people wanted the Ohio River established as the boundary line between the whites and Indians.

In 1788, white settlers began to move in west of the Ohio River, and the Indian tribes took up the warpath, spilling much blood on the frontier. Of course, the U.S. retaliated. An expedition of 1500 men was sent in 1789 under General Josiah Harmer, and a second one in 1791 under General Arthur St. Clair, with 2500 men. Both suffered crushing defeats. Most people have heard of Custer's defeat at the Little Big Horn, but not too much has ever been written about these great defeats of the U.S. military by our Lenapé under Buckongahelas, the Miami under Chief Little Turtle, and the Shawnee under Blue Jacket. A surprising fact concerning the Shawnee Chief Blue Jacket is that he was white, taken captive as a teenager!

In 1794, a third military expedition by the Americans under General "Mad" Anthony Wayne, with 5000 soldiers, finally defeated our Indian Confederacy at the Battle of Fallen Timbers along the Maumee River in Indiana.

In 1795, a peace treaty was signed by the Ohio Indian Tribes at Greenville, Ohio. By the terms of this treaty, we were to cease hostilities, give up white captives, acknowledge ourselves as under protection of the U.S., and we were given sole occupancy of the land west of the Cuyahoga River and south and west of the Great Lakes, as far as the Mississippi. The U.S. government agreed to protect us against any white intrusion, and we could only sell our land to the U.S.

Following the Treaty of Greenville, the Miami invited the Ohio tribes to settle in their Indiana Territory. By 1800, our Lenapé, Mahikani (Mohican) and Munsee peoples were well established

INTRODUCTION

on the White River. However, our people were greatly disheartened and alcoholism' had become widespread.

In the War of 1812, with the British and Americans doing battle, the English attempted to get us involved but we remained neutral.

Although numerous treaties had been negotiated with our Native peoples in Indiana Territory, in 1818 almost two-thirds of the young State of Indiana was still in the possession of the Indian Nations. This being so, the Americans could not settle there and this was a deterrent to white expansion. However, due to the growing white population, more land was needed, and so a growing populace urged the government to extinguish our claims to our land.

Thus our people were coerced into signing a treaty Oct. 3, 1818, at St. Mary's, Ohio. By the terms of this treaty we Lenapé agreed to give up our occupancy rights to all lands in Indiana. By 1821 most of our people had been moved to the western bank of the Mississippi.

1829 saw us enter into another treaty, in which we were granted new lands in eastern Kansas. We moved there from where we were settled on the James Fork of the White River in Missouri. We became a plains people, hunting buffalo, and we were often at war with the Osage and Pawnee, whose lands we were forced onto. In 1831 we were again moved to a new reservation on the north bank of the Kansas River.

In 1854 our people signed the Manypenny Treaty. Through this we were coerced into selling a lot of our land and we had to give up even more in 1860 and 1864.

Finally, in 1866, we entered into another treaty that called for our people to remove themselves to Indian territory in Oklahoma on the Cherokee Reservation. The descendants of those people are to be found there to this day.

So, it was a long trail of tears for many of our people. We were once a great and proud people, and are now reduced almost to nothing. We had to face all the problems that the reservation would bring forth. Our culture and traditions almost died out, our spirituality became almost extinct, and in 1993 there was only one fluent Lenapé speaker left alive.

31

However, though most of our people left the east, in our original lands of Lenape'hokink, there were many who intermarried with whites, or who continued to live in the east in small, rural communities. These people, my ancestors among them, were those who stayed behind and absorbed themselves into white society. This was true also in all of the lands that we had settled in, in Pennsylvania, Ohio and Indiana. The descendants of these, who stayed behind and never migrated west, are still here today; we have never left.

Today, here in the east, we the descendants of those who stayed behind have come together as tribes once again, and we are working very hard to bring back the culture, traditions and spirituality of our ancestors. However, as tribes, we have no Federal recognition, since our ancestors never went to a reservation; thus the U.S. government doesn't give us any support. We, the Eastern Lenapé, far outnumber our relatives on the Oklahoma Reservation, and for the most part are non-Christian and very traditional; we follow as best we can in the footsteps of our forefathers.

LENAPÉ SPIRITUALITY

Contrary to longstanding popular opinion, Native spirituality is not a godless religion. There are many Native religions, but they all have similar practices and beliefs. I will not get into any such comparisons here, but will discuss only our Lenapé beliefs.

We Lenapé believe in a multitude of worlds, inhabited by spiritual beings or Spirits, who we Lenapé call *Manìto'wàk*. All of these different worlds, or circles of being, are here altogether within and behind each other, occupying the same space, together making a whole. One may compare them to an onion, composed of its many layers, circles within circles making up the whole, and you will be as close to a true understanding as is possible for our merely human minds.

We Lenapé recognize three principal divisions of the spiritual whole of the universe, using the Earth as the center point of our thinking. There are twelve worlds above, in the Place Above the Earth, the Upper Spirit Worlds; then, there is the physical world of the Earth—the physical universe, and everything that we can see, hear and touch; and there also exist the numerous worlds in the Place Under the Earth, the Underworld.

Our Creator, Kishelamàkânk, we hold to live in the uppermost world, the highest level of heavenly light, the center of creation, and also the whole. We hold the Creator to have had no beginning and no end. He exists throughout all things and everything is but an expression of his great thought and power. Thus, we believe that all things have spirit, are innately alive, and can exert influences on the things around them. Everything that exists partakes of the power of the Creator, some having more or less and some being good and some bad. Everything is gifted to a greater or lesser degree and able to share or confer this spiritual power to we human beings, to help us in our lives in many ways.

In the Place Above the Earth, there exists what is called the spirit world, the Land of Spirits or Souls. We call this Awâsakame, the Land Beyond. It is as a mirror to the physical world—there is no death, war, pain or sorrow there, all is good, all is beautiful and peaceful. This is where the Spirits of those who have lived good lives go, holding goodness and peace in their hearts, walking along the Star Path, the White or Beautiful Path (the Milky Way), to get there. Along the Path to that place is a fork, watched by our Keeper Grandmother, a Spirit who only allows those of good spirit to enter into the Land of Souls. Those who have not learned their lessons in life, or have not strived towards good in their lives, who have left life too soon, committed suicide, sought power over others or to do harm to others, these travel along the other fork and enter the river between life and death, between this world and the world of Spirit. Many reincarnate, living again until they learn their lessons in Spirit, purifying their Spirits with good hearts. Others become lost and wander endlessly, bringing sickness and disease and much harm to the living.

Many people are under the mistaken notion that we worship the Sun, Moon, Earth, etc. This is not true, for we worship only the Creator, but recognize the Spirits who help him, honoring them in thanksgiving and prayer. Below are some of the powerful Manìto'wàk in Nature, who we honor.

The Spirit of the Sun, whom we call Nux Kishux, our Father Sun, who gives forth light, heat, love and life to all the Earth. The Sun teaches us generosity, it is always giving, but never asks for anything in return. We should strive to be happy and cheerful, bright like the Sun.

The Moon, the first Mother, who we Eastern Lenapé call Nipahuma, "Grandmother who goes by night," she who travels at night in the river of stars. Grandmother Moon gives life, fertility and the power of reproduction. The Oklahoma, Western Lenapé, hold the Moon to be male. However, originally, here in the east, the Moon was seen as female.

The Earth, we call Kukna, our Mother. All life arises from her and is nourished from her breast. She carries all life upon her. The rocks are her bones, the winds her breath, and the waters her life's blood. We see her as a great, living, breathing being.

At the four directions are four Great Spirit Beings who control the Universe, the Keepers of the Creation, and helpers of the Great Spirit (Creator):

In the North, is our Grandfather, Muxumsa Lowànewànk, who gave forth solidity and physical being to the whole of creation. He brings forth the winter, ice, frost and cold with his helper, Snow Boy. North Grandfather teaches us patience and endurance, and gives us strength, wisdom and purity. He has given to us our bodies and everything that we see around us.

In the East, is our Grandfather, Muxumsa Wapànewànk, who brought forth the winds, the air we breathe, who gave us breath that we might live. He brings forth the Sun at the start of each new day, and is the Spirit of birth and new beginnings. Bringing forth the light of the Sun, he gives us knowledge, our minds, creativity and illumination.

Wapalànito is a Spirit-helper for East Grandfather, who in the guise of the hawk or eagle sees everything that happens upon the Earth. Nothing escapes his gaze, and he can see into our hearts and know our minds. He is a messenger to the Spirits above, taking our thoughts and prayers to the World Above, that they might be heard.

In the South, is our Grandmother, Huma Shawánewànk, who is the Spirit behind heat, warmth and fire, giving an inner fire to all life. Maturity and growth are her gifts to all things, and also love, faith and trust. Grandfather Fire is her helper to us, giving us the gift of fire to cook our food, to keep us warm and to give us light when it is dark.

In the West, is our Grandfather, Muxumsa Wunchènewànk, who controls the waters of the Earth, who gives us our life's blood, who gives us dreams and vision, gives us our emotions and who brings us healing. The Thunderers, Pethakowe'jàk, are West Grandfather's helpers, bringing the rains which nourish the Earth and give water to all life, who watch over our sacred objects and ceremonies, and who bring warnings to humankind.

There is a Spirit who we call Misinkhâlikàn, the Masked Being. He is the Guardian of the Forest, who watches over the trees and takes care of the game and other animals, providing food for humankind. Many people know him as "Bigfoot" or "Sasquatch," often seen as a great hairy ape-like creature, eight to ten feet tall, that leaves quite a strong odor. Misink can enter this world, be seen, leave footprints, and be gone at his whim. He often uses a body of water or trees as doorways to the Spirit World. Usually he is seen in areas that are being logged or where housing developments are built in wilderness areas. Often his physical presence is a message, that we are out of balance with Nature or acting disharmoniously with respect to the natural world around us. We give prayers and tobacco offerings to Misinkhâlikàn before entering the forest or before we go hunting.

Another Spirit, Mother Corn, Kahesana Xaskwim, controls the vegetation, the trees and plants, and who gives us an abundance of crops, berries, fruits and nuts to provide us with food.

We also know Spirits of the stars, mountains, the rocks, the waters, and there are the Little People, who we call Wematekàn'is, or Wood Dwarfs. Indeed, the Creator has many who help him in keeping a harmonious balance throughout creation.

Whereas the Creator is continuously creating, there is another

Spirit, called Matantu, who resides in the Underworld and is an opposing, balancing force in the Universe. Sometimes he is destructive, negative and evil in his actions. But he is not like the Christian Devil, but rather like the Chinese concept of yin and yang, or opposing, balancing forces. Thus, there is good and evil, day and night, male and female, positive and negative. Without the opposite forces found in Nature, the Universe would cease to be and fall apart. Matantu often brings us bad thoughts and dreams, and often tests our Spirits.

There are many Spirits of an evil nature, who seek to control and manipulate people, and cause harm or bring sickness to us. Other Spirits, often called Tricksters, play pranks on people, and often come to teach us lessons. Then there are the Chipe'wàk, Spirits of the Dead, of those who have gone before us. Some are Spirits that are not at rest, who seek to bring harm and sickness; but there are others who have left this world in peace, who reach out into our world and into our lives, to help us and to guide us in times of trouble and need.

Guardian Spirits are those Spirits who help us, guide us and empower us, giving us good fortune and good health. These are sought after and received upon undergoing a fasting quest. They often give us medicines to help us in our lives or in what we are to do, and often come to heal and protect us. They usually appear in animal form or partake of some natural phenomena such as hail, clouds, etc. We make medicine bags or bundles containing a physical part or some representation of our Guardian Spirits and keep this on our person, to receive the blessings from these Spirits and to keep a strong connection to it, so that its power may do its work in our lives.

At the center of our spirituality is Thanksgiving, Kenama'kàn. We give thanks and prayer, morning and evening, giving thanks for our lives, for all that enters our lives, for our families, friends and health and well-being. Before we eat or drink we always give thanks for the food that nourishes us and the water that sustains us and all life. We recognize that there is much to be thankful for, and we humble ourselves before the Creator and all of creation, as we are so dependent on so many things for our very lives.

INTRODUCTION

Our spirituality is as simple as it is complex. Whereas Christianity is a religion of faith, our religion is based on experience, through observing and living close to Nature. We have no book such as a Bible. Our Bible is in the Sun, Moon, mountains, sky, trees and the living world around us, and in the wisdom passed down to us from our ancestors on the tongues of our Elders and Wise and Holy Ones.

Whereas Christianity teaches that man is favored by God over all life, our belief is that we are but a part of the world, of no greater or superior importance than anything else. It is not hard to see that all life would do just fine without us.

Prayer is also an important part of our lives, and this is done morning and night, individually. We pray for our lives, for all life, and for those who have need. During ceremonies, when we come together, we pray together, for our people, and for each other, sending our thoughts to the Creator and the Spirits upon the smoke from burning tobacco, either in a fire or a pipe (even a cigarette may suffice). Tobacco, as discussed above, is a medium through which our prayers are directed, our thoughts and prayers rising with the smoke of the burning tobacco to the World of Spirits, that they may be heard.

Offerings of tobacco are given whenever we wish to show respect, to please and gain the blessings of the Spirits. Thus, we offer tobacco to our crops, that they will grow and provide us with food that we may live; to any animals that we may kill; to the Spirits of the forests before we enter therein or go hunting; for protection, before embarking on a trip or journey, or when traveling by water; or anytime that we cut down a live tree or pick herbs and plants for our needs.

Purification is an important part of our spirituality, and is done in one of three ways:

Through smudging, cleansing by smoke, of ourselves or objects, especially medicine (spiritual) objects or items. The smoke is produced by burning herbs on hot coals, using pine cones, pine resins, sage, white or red cedar, or sweetgrass. Such smoke is directed with a feather over a person or object, the smoke that is produced cleaning the person or object of all negative and evil influences, bad thoughts or bad/evil Spirits.

Another way of cleansing-purification is through fasting. This is often done before entering into anything of a spiritual nature, enabling one to become more of a clear channel, a clear and pure vessel for Spirit. Fasting is especially done before healing work, a sweatlodge or when a vision quest is undertaken. Fasting purifies by cleansing the body, and thus cleansing the heart, mind and Spirit. Fasting can be done as a personal sacrifice to gain pity and help from the Spirits with some undertaking, or when healing is desired or when there is a real need to be met. Sometimes fasting is done when protesting something we strongly disagree with or in remembrance of a person or event.

The sweatlodge is the supreme method of cleansing, for healing or purification of body, heart, mind and Spirit, especially when combined with fasting. We call the sweatlodge, Pimâ'kàn, coming from our word *pìm* "to sweat." The sweatlodge is part of the original instructions given to us by the Creator. Some think that the sweatlodge is like a sauna, but it is a religious ceremony and is actually much hotter. The sweatlodge is dome-shaped, made of bent poles, 9 to 12 feet in diameter, and covered over with whatever we happen to have on hand, blankets, tarps, plastic, bark, boards, earth, etc. A fire is built, rocks are heated red hot and brought inside the lodge and then water is poured on them, creating very hot steam. In the old days there were separate men's and women's sweatlodges, usually at opposite ends of the village. However, the sweatlodge is basically a men's ceremony, as women are seen to have a natural, built-in sweatlodge cleansing during their Moontime or menstrual period. Thus, women don't really need to partake of a sweatlodge cleansing; but men, lacking this natural process, use the sweatlodge. However, due to the polluted state of the environment nowadays, our women too make regular use of it. Women who had reached menopause traditionally used the sweatlodge, as they had lost their natural menstruating/cleansing ability. Women who were involved in medicine societies and healing practices also took the sweatlodge.

In our sweatlodge ceremony, our bodies are cleansed through sweating; our emotions and minds are cleansed by releasing pent-up feelings and thoughts through singing, crying, or fervent prayer; and our Spirits are cleansed by the fire in the rocks and the steam.

This ceremony consists of four parts: the first, singing sacred songs, inviting the spirits to be with us, a thanksgiving address and giving individual thanks; the second part involves the singing of healing songs received from Spirits for the healing of ourselves; in the third part, prayers are given for healing and helping others in need; and in the fourth, we seek vision and guidance, using a rattle to loosen our Spirits and meditation-like techniques.

The most important spiritual undertaking of our people is the vision quest, or *linkwehèlan*. Our young men, when they are 14 or 15 years old, make preparations for a fasting quest, alone in the forest, undergoing prior purification, and praying for a vision. We believe that a man is nothing without vision. Until one has a vision one merely exists; but having vision brings one alive, giving meaningful purpose and direction to one's life. Upon receiving a vision, we then seek to fulfill this. Now, we believe that women are naturally fulfilled in their purpose, that is to have children, to raise and nurture them, and thus they don't really need to seek a vision. However, if a woman feels the need to or desires to, she may also seek for vision on a fasting quest. Usually a woman would do this in a *wiktut* (menstrual lodge) upon the start of her Moontime. The vision quest guides a person to their path in life, teaches them their duty before the Creator, gives them medicines to protect, help and guide them, gives them Guardian Spirit(s), and blesses them with a sacred name. The vision quest is most important, for it gives us a sense of who we are, makes us aware of the purpose of our lives, and gives us a greater understanding of all that exists around us, and of our place in the Circle of Life.

Our spiritual leaders, our medicine people, our holy ones, are guided to such a calling through vision. There are several ways that one might be guided onto the path of medicine, as a prophet, a healer, a seer, a sweatlodge doctor, an herbalist, a pipe carrier, one who works with fire, etc., according to the contents of one's vision. Often medicine people are specialized in a certain area, for example in locating missing or lost persons or objects, or they may be gifted in two or more areas.

Our medicine people are highly respected, for they heal the sick, teach us our spirituality (religion), counsel people with problems, and usually are blessed with the gift of speaking to the Spirits and bringing back wisdom and knowledge to help the people in their lives. Medicine people lead our spiritual ceremonies, calling the Spirits to be with us, bringing harmony to all land and life, and blessings upon the people. To approach a medicine person, one brings to them a gift of tobacco, and then states one's reason for seeking help.

Our spirituality is interwoven and surrounds our lives, and is deep in meaning for us. It is not something separate from our lives, or just put to use one day a week, but is utilized on a day to day basis in many different ways.

STORIES AND STORYTELLING

Native American stories bring alive our values and morals and our way of life. They teach us, our children and others about our culture and traditions, serving to show that we too are people with feelings, dreams, wishing a good future for our children, and that we have a place here in the world, that we do exist. Indeed, there is much about our traditional lifeways that could be adopted by the modern world to put an end to many of the troubles, such as pollution and war, that beset us today; to ensure that our children may continue to live into the future. All of this can be shown in our stories. They can teach us about relationships, between ourselves and others, between humankind, the animals, plants, and the spirit beings, showing us our dependence as human beings upon all land and life upon our Mother Earth. They tell not only of ourselves and our relationship to the places in which we live, but also teach us our origins, about our ancestors, who we are and where we come from. Stories give us solid roots from which to grow and give direction to our future generations, our children and our children's children.

Our stories may embody several concepts of our philosophy, spirituality, and our lifeways. Native American stories are not meant to be taken in a literal or rigid and gospel-like manner. As you read the stories, as you listen to them, it is expected that you make your own interpretations, and draw your own conclusions as to the meanings within them. Perhaps they may have a message just for you at this time in your life, and maybe when reading them at a later time you may see something else. There is a strong Native belief in not interfering with others, but instead in giving them the chance to have their own thoughts, to make up their own minds and express themselves freely.

Storytelling to us is a community experience, a coming together of people, to share in our past, our way of life, and in and of ourselves as a people. The contents of stories at times may seem fantastic, but storytelling is not intended just for children. When a story is told, people of all ages gather around, experiencing the other realities and worlds of the story, connecting us with that child-like wonder within us all, opening us up to limitless possibilities and setting free our minds to imagine and to see wonder in the world around us.

We Lenapé have several different terms we can use to categorize stories: *enèndàkewa'kàn*—a parable, these teach us lessons; *klakàptâna'kàn*—an amusing story; *lachimosuwa'kàn*—a story of something in life, past or present; *atiloha'kàn*—a story that explains natural phenomena, stories of the Spirits, the Creation, etc. (these are gospel-like, they never change, and are held to be very sacred).

Among my Lenape'wàk, stories were only told at certain times of the year. The time for storytelling began with the first frost and ended with the last frost. They were told only in the wintertime and around an open fire. Stories were not to be told in the summer because there are many creatures around who might take offence at stories being told about them and take revenge on the Storyteller, or they might tell some powerful Spirit, who could come and cause trouble. Also, the Wematekàn'is, the Little People, are always listening in the forest. If they hear a story being told about them, they may turn into an insect, snake, or other creature, that may come to you and bite, sting, or do you harm. So, we tell our stories in the wintertime, when all of the troublemaking and mischievous beings are asleep.

41

THE GRANDFATHERS SPEAK

We also believe that if you tell stories in the summertime when the crops are growing, the corn, beans, squash, etc. may stop to listen to you and forget their duties—to grow and produce. It is believed that stories are so powerful that things in Nature will listen to them and get confused, and forget what it is that they are supposed to do. The only stories that are to be told in summertime are histories, biographies, or the Creation Story and those like it of a sacred nature, which may be told in connection with certain spiritual ceremonies.

Stories are at their best when they are narrated. With skill and imagination a Storyteller, Lachimo, can make a story come alive and put the audience into another reality, forgetting this world and living for a while in the world of the story.

Our Lachimochik (Storytellers) traveled from village to village during the winter, telling stories. Upon entering a village, a Storyteller would be invited to tell his stories, gifts would be given, and food and shelter provided for him. Storytellers were regarded as bringers of good luck. Our old stories were considered the greatest of gifts given to us. They hold powerful medicine and are to be treated with the utmost respect, as are those who tell them.

So, now, sit and relax, and enter with me into the world of the stories of my Lenape'wàk. Come with me now into the mists of time, it is winter, it is cold, and there is much snow . . .

The Storyteller walks down the river valley now, after having spent a few days at a small village upstream, telling stories and partaking of the generosity and hospitality of the villagers. A few young warriors escort him in his journey downriver a few miles to another village. Though the snow is deep, the going is easy with the help of snowshoes. The warriors escort him to provide him with protection, to see that he gets safely to his destination. For the Storyteller is considered to be very special, bringing good luck and the powerful medicine of his stories to the people. Lachimo, the Storyteller, keeps the lifeways of the people alive through the telling of his stories, bringing the customs and traditions to bear on the minds of the young and old alike.

Upon reaching the next village, he is greeted warmly and openly, being excitedly expected by everyone. He is invited to spend the night in the *wikwàm* of the Chief, and to eat with his family. So he goes there, enters, is introduced to all in the household, and is given a bowl of food to eat. After he is finished eating he is given a place to rest, for it is clear that he is tired from his journey.

When he awakes from his sleep it is now evening, just beginning to get dark outside, so he eats some food which is offered to him, and then he prepares in silence, alone, for what he has come for, to tell the stories to the people.

The Chief interrupts his contemplation, inviting him to the Council House. The Storyteller follows the Chief, and is led to a long bark-covered building which he enters; he sits down before the fire. People are coming from the whole village, and they gather around the large fire with him.

The grandmothers and mothers are telling the children to be on their best behavior in the presence of the Lachimo. They are told not to interrupt him at any time or to leave while he is speaking, and that they may ask questions after each story or may then leave to play for a bit. If these things are not followed, the Storyteller may become angry at such disrespect and refuse to tell any more stories. Bad luck may come as a result of such rude behavior.

Everyone has gathered round now, all is quiet, and the Storyteller begins. First, as always, he tells the story that began all stories, Kishelamàwa'kàn, the Story of the Creation. "*Kàlès'ta!* Listen!" he says. "*Kunakwat, lowat, nuchink* .... Long, long ago, in the beginning ..." It is a long story, and a few times during its telling he says, "*Kàlès'ta!* Listen! Ho!*" to keep the attention of those around him who are listening. Finally the Storyteller says, "*Juke lachimu kishaloke!* .... Now the story is finished!" The people are saying, "*Wanishi!* Thank you! *Wulihìle!* It is good!"

Some people get up to stretch, others are asking questions, some children go out to play and the women talk. The men fill their pipes to smoke, the smoke from each pipe mingling together into one smoke, symbolizing the coming together of the people and their thoughts, bringing the Spirits near to them, to listen and give them blessings. A child shouts, "Tell us another!

THE GRANDFATHERS SPEAK

Tell us another! *Kàtèlinin ta'kàn! Kàtèlinin ta'kàn!"* Another child follows quickly repeating the cry, then another. The women admonish the children saying, *"Se he! Se he!* Hush! Hush!" The Storyteller looks on amused, a smile on his face.

Now, the Storyteller says, *"Kàlès'ta!* Listen!" Everyone gives their attention to him respectfully, and all is quiet.

The Lachimo puts his hand into a deerskin bag at his side. It is decorated with dyed porcupine quills and deer hair with figures of men and animals. Inside his story bag (*lachimume-nu'tez*) are mnemonic devices, natural objects (acorns, feathers, etc.) and carved figures, which serve to represent different stories. Now the Lachimo grabs onto the first object he feels in his story bag. It is an acorn, representing a tale of the Little People, the Wematekàn'is. So, he begins his tale . . . but it is short and it is not long before he is heard to say, *"Juke lachimu kishaloke!* Now, the story is finished!"

The people are laughing, for this story was very funny! The people give thanks, saying, *"Wanishi!* Thank you! *Wulilisap!* It was good!" The children are saying, *"Lapixsi!* Tell it over again!" Again, the women admonish the children, *"Se he!* Hush!" The Storyteller smiles, for a story is only told once; there are many more to tell.

The tales continue on through the night and occasionally the Lachimo can be heard to say, "Ho! *Kàlès'ta!* Listen!", to keep the people alert. But finally some begin to drift off to sleep and the Storyteller knows it is time to stop for now. *"Juke nishix'ten!* Now, I am finished!" he tells them.

There are more tales to be told, but these must wait for another night. . . .

So, some night, gather your family and friends around near you. Become the Storyteller, say, "Ho! *Kàlès'ta!* Listen!", and share with them these stories of my Lenapé people, stories from this land we call Amankitaxkwâwikan'ànk, the Place of the Great Turtle's Back.

Xinkwishùmánk (Place of the Big Horn)
Hitakonanulaxk (Tree Beard)

THE LENAPÉ CREATION
(LENAPÉ KISHELAMÀWA'KÀN)

Our *lèpâ'chik*, wise ones, say: *"Kunakwat, lowat, nuchink....*
Long, long ago, in the beginning..." at first there was only
endless space, and therein dwelt Kishelamàkânk, the Creator.
Nothing else existed at this time, all was silence and there was
a great peace.

Then it was that Kishelamàkânk had a great vision. In this
vision he saw the endless space around him filled with stars,
and he saw the sun, the moon, and the Earth. On the Earth he
saw mountains, valleys, lakes, rivers, and forests. He saw the
trees, flowers, crops and grasses, and the crawling, walking,
swimming and flying beings. He saw the birth of things, their
growth and death, and other things that apparently lived forever. Then he heard songs, stories, laughs and cries. The Creator touched the wind and the rain, felt love and hate, courage
and fear, happiness and sorrow. Then the vision passed, and it
was gone!

Kishelamàkânk, the Creator, had seen that which was unknown, and he thought deeply upon all that he had seen in his
vision. He came to understand that the vision would come into
being. When there was nothing around him but empty space,
his mind saw nothing and so nothing was created. Now, through
thought, thinking in his mind of the vision, it started to happen.

There were first created the Keepers of Creation, four powerful Spirit Beings, to help him in his task of fulfilling and creating the vision: the Spirits of Rock, Fire, Wind and Water. Into
each he breathed life and Spirit, giving to each different characteristics and powers. These four beings were:

Muxumsa Lowànewànk, our Grandfather in the North. He was

placed there to control the power of rock. He gave forth solidity and physical form to the Creator's thought, to his vision. North Grandfather gives us the wintertime, ice, snow and cold; also, our bodies, the rocks, the trees, and all that we see around us;

Muxumsa Wapànewànk, our Grandfather in the East. He was placed there to control the power of the wind. He gave forth breath and mind to the Creator's vision. He gives us the spring-time, the breath of life, birth and new beginnings, and brings forth the light, the winds, our minds, creativity, knowledge, music and songs;

Huma Shawànewànk, our Grandmother in the South. She was placed there to control the power of fire. She gave forth Spirit, life and growth to the vision of the Creator. She gives us the summer, warmth, growth and maturity, our inner fire and Spirit, and gives fire to the sun;

Muxumsa Wunchènewànk, our Grandfather in the West. He was placed there to control the power of water. He brought a watery and softening influence to the Creator's vision. He gives us the autumn, gives us death, and readies us for renewal, and gave us the waters, our life's blood, healing, intuition, emotions, dreams and visions, and rain.

These four Spirit beings, Keepers of the Creation, did help the Creator to make the stars, the sun, the moon and the Earth.

Now the Creator instructed all of these Beings to come to-gether on the Earth, to give of their powers together to create life. Nux Kishux, our Father Sun, gave heat and light, and Nipahuma, our Grandmother Moon, came down to Earth and gave of her powers of fertility and reproduction. Kukna, the Mother Earth, upon which life was to be born, gave growth and healing. North Grandfather gave form to all life, East Grand-father gave the breath of life and Spirit, South Grandmother gave inner fire and Spirit, and West Grandfather gave of its water to life, life's blood.

First were made the plant beings of four kinds, grasses, flower-ing plants, trees, and crops. To each was given, through Spirit, life, growth, healing, and beauty. Each was placed where it would be most useful, and give the greatest harmony and balance to all land and life.

THE LENAPÉ CREATION

Then were made the animal beings. Each being was given special powers and characteristics. There were those that crawled and walked upon the Earth, those that swam in the lakes, rivers, and streams upon the good Earth, and those that flew in the skies above.

Now, Nipahuma, our Grandmother Moon, having been set in the night sky, her Spirit became lonely and so she asked the Creator for a companion. The Creator sent her a Spirit, Grandfather Thunder, Muxumsa Pethakowe, to keep her company. With him she conceived, and when she came to lend her powers of fertility to the Earth to help in the creation of life, she gave birth upon the Earth to twins—one a man, and the other a woman. Thus it was that humankind was the last of beings created. Though they were different, man and woman found a wholeness in union with each other. Only together were they complete and fulfilled, only together could they fulfill their purpose. The Creator gave man and woman a special gift, the power to dream. Nipahuma, our Mother who goes by night, the first mother, the mother of all mothers, nurtured her children, and then when her purpose was complete she returned to the spirit world; but before she left she told first man and woman that she would never forget them. She continues to watch over us at night as the Moon. The children promised to remember Grandmother Moon whenever she appeared in the sky, giving her light to guide our paths.

In vision the Creator had seen things of opposite natures, and so was created light and darkness, male and female, hot and cold, above and below, good and evil. Where the Creator created, giving forth goodness and light, Matantu, a Spirit of destruction, evil and darkness came into being. Where the Creator made edible plants, Matantu made poisonous plants. Where the Creator made the delicious blackberries, Matantu put thorns on them. Matantu also made tormenting insects such as flies, mosquitoes and poisonous snakes.

Many such laws were woven into the creation by Kishela-màkânk, the Creator, for the well-being, harmony and balance of all things and all creatures. These laws gave place and motion to the sun, moon, Earth and stars, and governed the powers of wind, water, fire and rock, and the circle of life, birth, growth and death. All things existed and worked through these laws. The Creator's vision was now brought into being.

Now, upon the newly formed Earth, the Creator put a Spirit Being, Kichichax'kàl, the Great Toad, who was given the duty of ruling over the waters of the Earth. He was given the authority, and the power, to cause rain to fall at his will, and was also known as Bikanaki'hàt, the Water Keeper.

One day, Maxa'xâk, an evil Manìto (Spirit) appeared, who came to bother and quarrel with the Great Toad. This evil Spirit had the form of a vicious and ugly horned serpent. Maxa'xâk, the horned serpent, fought with Kichichax'kàl, the Great Toad, because he wanted to be the one to rule over the waters of the Earth. One day they fought such a terrible battle that it caused a great disturbance over the whole new Earth. The Great Toad tried to swallow the evil snake, but the monster snake gored the Great Toad so severely that he died. And the four winds, *newakishe'na*, the mighty seas, and all the waters of the Earth, lashed out in everlasting fury at the evil serpent, but all to no avail.

Now, Kishelamàkânk, the Creator of all things, saw the struggle, the turmoil, the steadily growing unrest, and he sent the Thunder Spirit to battle the horned serpent, Maxa'xâk. Grandfather Thunder came swiftly, announcing his arrival by the sound of his bone rattles, and shooting his lightning arrows, forcing the evil serpent to flee. The rain fell, the waters rose and gushed forth everywhere, washing away the corruption and evil that had covered the blood-stained Earth. The rising waters caused widespread destruction upon the Earth, which became one great sea. Many plants and animals died, and all of humankind perished due to the destruction wrought by the evil serpent.

Now, Maxa'xâk and his children stay put in the watery depths, fearing the Thunderers who pursue them when they dare to venture forth, shooting their lightning arrows at the evil snakes.

At this time, there was another Spirit Being also on the Earth, the Wise and Gifted Being called Nanapush, the Strong Pure One, the Grandfather of Beings and Men. When he saw the rapidly rising water, he sought refuge on the highest mountain, hoping that there he would be safe. But the rain fell and fell, and the waters continued to rise, until at last there was left only a small patch of ground on top of the highest mountain. And upon the top of this mountain, there was growing a small cedar tree. The rain continued, coming down in torrents for many days. It was now apparent that all of the seven islands, and the mountains, would soon be entirely covered with water. So the great and wise Nanapush picked up the animals and birds that had gathered on the mountain-top, and he tucked them carefully and safely inside his shirt. Then he went to the cedar tree, and spoke to it before he started to climb it. As he climbed he broke off branches and put them under his belt. Soon he reached the top of the tree, but the waters continued to rise and rise, now almost to his feet. So the great Nanapush began to sing and beat on his bow-string which served as a drum. As he sang, the cedar tree, the sacred tree, began to grow and grow, and it kept on growing as the waters continued to rise. After a long time, Nanapush, the Strong Pure One, the Grandfather of Beings and Men, grew tired of singing his song of peace to the raging elements, so he threw upon the waters the branches which he had plucked as he climbed. At once they took the form of a strong raft. On this raft he carefully placed all of the creatures he had saved, and they floated upon the waters on the cedar raft. Soon he saw all the mountain peaks disappear under the steadily rising water; only Nanapush and the creatures he had saved remained alive.

After some time, Nanapush decided a new Earth should be made, a task he could well perform through the powers granted to him by the Creator. So he held a Council with the little creatures and they went to work to help him form a new island. Their first duty would be to get some soil from the submerged Earth. The first one to offer his help was Mitewile'un, the Loon. He dived and stayed down a very long time. When he came floating back up to the surface he was dead. So the great Nanapush breathed upon the unfortunate Loon, and its life was restored. Now Kùna'moxk, the Otter, dived down, but he failed in the attempt and also came up dead; he too was restored to life by Nanapush. Then Tamakwa, the Beaver, tried, but he in turn failed and had to be revived. Then Nanapush turned to Tamask'was, the Muskrat, and told him that he must try very hard to reach the old Earth. The little Muskrat stayed down twice as long as any of the rest, and he came to the surface completely exhausted, but still alive. And in his mouth and paws he carried some of the precious mud from the old world below the waters. The great Nanapush was pleased, and he carefully revived the little Muskrat and blessed him, promising him that his kind would never die out.

Now Nanapush made a great ceremony, a thanksgiving ceremony, the first thanksgiving ceremony ever to take place. Then, Nanapush called for a helper who would receive and carry the new Earth. Taxkwâx, the Turtle, responded and was at once chosen to perform this important duty. Nanapush placed the mud brought back by Tamask'was, the Muskrat, upon the back of the Turtle, and blew his life-giving breath into it. Immediately it began to grow; it grew and grew until it became the great island where all of us are living today. Because Turtle carried the new Earth on his back, this is why this land upon which we live is called Taxkwâx Mènâ'te, Turtle Island, and Amankitaxkwâwikan'ànk, the Place of the Great Turtle's Back.

For his help, Taxkwâx, the Turtle, became the messenger of thoughts and feeling between different beings. A symbol of thought given and received, representing communication between all things.

After some time had passed, Nanapush sent Tàme, the Wolf, to see how large the new Earth had grown. The first time Wolf went on his journey, he was gone for one day. The second time he went he was gone five days; the next, ten days; then, one moon; next, one year; then, five years; then again, for twelve years. The next time he went, he never returned, but became lost on the great wide Earth and died of old age. That is why today, at every full moon, the wolves sit in the forest howling, in remembrance of the great misfortune suffered by their ancestor long ago.

When Tàme, the Wolf, failed to return, Nanapush, the Strong Pure One, the Grandfather of Beings and Men, decided that the new Earth was now large enough, so he commanded it to stop growing.

As the waters subsided, the animal beings brought grasses,

flowers, trees and food-bearing plants to Nanapush. Into each he breathed life and restored them on their island home.

Then the Earth was dry, and good to look upon. Indeed, it was very beautiful, and there grew a pale and lovely tree from the Mother Earth, and the root of this new tree sent forth a sprout beside it. After a time there grew upon it a man, the first on the new Earth. This man was there alone, and may have remained there alone forever, but the shimmering tree bent over its top to kiss the Mother Earth. Where the tree had touched the Earth, there appeared another sprout, and there grew the first woman of the new Earth.

The wise ones tell us that from those two beings, that man and woman, came our Lenape'wàk, Lenapé people, owing our origin and faithfulness to the shimmering tree and the good Mother Earth.

Now on the new Earth, first man and first woman were nourished by food and drink brought by the animals, our elder brothers. The birds brought song and dance, the butterflies and bees amusement. All the animal beings served in some way except Màka'na, the Dog. Being less gifted than other animals, he had nothing to offer, but felt he must give something. So, the dog pledged his love, and lay down beside where first man and first woman were sleeping. From that day the dog has remained by the side of humankind.

The first winter was a difficult one for those first Lenapé. The weather was very bad and the animals found food hard to find for them. So, Maxkwe, the Bear, fearing their death, offered of himself that they might live. With Bear's flesh they survived, and thereafter the other animals gave of themselves, their lives, to feed human beings. In gratitude and honor of the sacrifice of Bear, our ancestors held special ceremonies of thanksgiving for the gift of life from Bear and the other animals. We survive and have life because of the deaths of our elder brothers.

Nanapush taught our Lenape'wàk how to make everything we would need to live, the making of clothing, homes, canoes; he taught us the principles of leadership, that we should not strive for power and control over others; he taught us how to make weapons and how to defend ourselves; taught us our way of life and wisdom, how we should live our lives, in a way that is good, and taught us the greatest of virtues, generosity and kindness; he taught us how to hunt and fish, how to grow crops and harvest them, how to cook and keep food through the winter. Nanapush gave our Lenape'wàk sacred medicine bundles which were to give us spiritual power to help us in times of need, he gave us the ceremonies we were to observe, taught us healing and our spiritual ways, and the importance of dream and vision.

Then, when Nanapush was sure of their survival, he called our Lenape'wàk to him and told them he was leaving. He told them always to remember the things and ways of life he had taught them, for then they would always live in peace and harmony with all land and life. The Old Ones say that his Spirit is with us still, and that if there comes a time when this world should end, he will come again to help guide us into a new Earth.

Nanapush was directed by a dream to retire into the wide expanses of the barren lands to the north, where he was to make for himself a home. So, he changed himself into a rabbit, and left, never being seen again by our people. Since that time, our Lenape'wàk have never used the rabbit for food, as it is a symbol of the regeneration and continuing of life.

When Nanapush arrived in the far northern lands he found the peaceful silence and quiet contentment which he so much desired. There he built for himself a very large *wikwàm*, a house, made of ice and snow. Now, every winter, he sleeps like Maxkwe, the Bear, but before going to his bed of bearskins, he always smokes his pipe. So, the next time you see the pretty colored leaves on the trees in autumn and thick fog in the morning, you will know that Nanapush, the Great Being, Grandfather of Beings and Men, is smoking his pipe and preparing to take his long winter nap.

NANAPUSH

Nanapush, Grandfather of our Lenape'wàk and Spirit helper to the Creator here on the Earth, brought we Lenapé our culture, religion and traditions, and taught these things to us. It was he who put the mud from the old Earth upon the back of the turtle, and he breathed upon it, whereby it grew becoming this Turtle Island where we live this day. He taught us all that we know, that we might live and survive.

It is said that Nanapush was born of a woman and Muxumsa Wunchènewànk, the Grandfather Spirit in the West. Being the son of so powerful a Manìto (Spirit), it was not surprising that he too became possessed of a strong power, so that he was more like a Spirit than a man.

It was not long after his birth that his mother died. Rumor had it that she had been murdered by her husband. So, Nanapush grew up never knowing his mother. And, soon after his mother's death, his father left, going to the west in the greatest of sorrow and grief, and he never returned. It is said that the rain is West Grandfather's tears and the darkness and dreariness of storms an expression of his loss for his wife. Muxumsa Wunchènewànk, or Wunchène'kis as he was also called, knowing that he could not be a proper parent to Nanapush, left him to be raised by his *huma*, his grandmother. She raised him to be a fine young man, teaching him all that she could and instilling within him as much wisdom as she could.

As Nanapush grew older, he asked his grandmother about his father and his mother; but she would not tell him, saying, "Later, when you are older, my grandson."

Now growing into manhood he came to realize the extent of his powers. It was at this time that his grandmother told him of his mother and father, and she told him that his father was still alive, a powerful Spirit in the west. By this time he had also heard the many rumors telling of his mother's murder at the hands of his father. Nanapush was angry and could think only of avenging his mother's death by killing his father. So, one day, he prepared to leave for the west to look for his father, over the objections of his grandmother. He took only his bow, some arrows and his medicine bundle and traveled west, crossing the Namès Sipu, Mississippi River, and heading towards the Kichiwaxchuwa, the Great Mountains or Rockies.

Finally, after a period of many moons, he reached the Land of the Great Mountains. He was tired, and made a resting place under a large tree. He didn't know how to find his father or even what he looked like if he were to meet him. He pulled out his pipe to smoke and to think on this, when he heard a voice, "Nanapush, beware, beware! Your father is a great and powerful Manìto, a Spirit. He knows that you are here for his vision is great, and he knows that you seek to destroy him. Go to Mahalèsànk, the Flint Place, and gather some flint pieces and sharpen them. They have the power of fire within them. If your father tries to harm you, use the flint against him, as it is the only thing he fears. It will hurt him but it cannot destroy him."

The voice stopped and Nanapush looked around, but saw only a *papa'xès*, a woodpecker, on a tree which then flew away. He thought it must have been the woodpecker that warned him, and so he gave thanks to it for the advice. Then he went to Mahalèsànk, the Flint Place, and he gathered up some flint. As he was sharpening some pieces, he saw a large man who approached him saying, "I am your father, Wunchène'kis!" "And I am your son," said Nanapush, greeting him with respect, yet suspicious of him.

Wunchène'kis said, "I know that you have come to kill me to avenge your mother's death, but know the truth! You listen to lies, for I did not kill your mother! I loved her and I still grieve for her!"

"That's what you say!" said Nanapush. "Why should I believe you? Why did you run away and leave me unless you had something to hide, to feel guilty and ashamed for? You are no father of mine! A father loves his son and would not leave him! So I choose not to trust in your words, and tomorrow I will fight you!"

Wunchène'kis looked sadly at his son and said, "My son, you cannot see the truth of which I speak through the fog of your pain. So it is, as you wish, tomorrow we shall fight! You may harm me but you will never destroy me, and my injury or death would not bring back your mother or allow you to know her love."

So, the next day, Nanapush met his father in battle. Wunchène'kis fired arrows and Nanapush threw his flints. To this day there are arrowheads and flint pieces found on the ground all over this Turtle Island as the result of that conflict long ago. All day they fought, until they ran out of arrows and flints, and then they fought hand to hand. The battle was so great that the sky darkened from the rising dust and the Earth trembled and shook. Then it seemed that his father was getting the best of him, so Nanapush took out a flint that he had saved and slashed Wunchène'kis in the head, cutting him badly. Wunchène'kis said, "Enough my son, enough! You have great power and are my equal, but you cannot vanquish me, and I cannot defeat you. To go on is senseless. Let us have peace between us. I shall remain in the west as is my duty. Return to your home and fulfill your purpose. As a remembrance of this day and the resulting peace between us, I would like to give you this pipe. Take it with you, come to know it for what it is, for all its power, for peace and goodwill."

So, Nanapush accepted the pipe and thanked his father, and together they smoked that pipe and brought their hearts and minds together as one, resolving the differences between them. A great love grew between them after spending some time together; father and son had much to talk about. However, the time came for them to part, and Nanapush left, returning home to learn of his purpose and duty before the Creator.

Nanapush was most noted for his power of transformation. He could change instantly and at will into anything that he so desired. Although he could change his physical form, essentially he was a Spirit.

While Nanapush was among our Lenapé people he appeared as a man, and in this form he was accepted and understood. Our Lenapé people came to love him dearly, and for his teachings we honor him in our stories and memories to this day.

HOW THE PIPE CAME
TO THE LENAPÉ

Long, long ago, when Kukna, the Mother Earth, was young and the Native people were all one people, there arose a great dispute among them concerning a sacred medicine, the tooth of a certain monster bear.

A Council fire burned for many days and many nights, but no agreement could be reached concerning this, and the people found it impossible to settle their differences or to come to a compromise. After countless debates and meetings, it was finally decided to separate into independent groups. So it was, that many clans and families went their separate ways. In time, many new tribes came into being, speaking new and different tongues and living in different ways.

Now it was that a certain gifted being, called Nanapush, a Spirit helper on this Earth to Kishelamàkânk, the Creator, the Grandfather of human beings and all living creatures, saw that his grandchildren, the Lenapé, the Grandfathers of men, were in great distress, that they were quarreling and drifting apart, and he felt a deep and sincere compassion for them.

So he asked Kishelamàkânk, the Creator of all things: "Kishelamìlenk, oh great Creator, I ask of your counsel. My Lenapé grandchildren need help, for they are deeply troubled." The Creator replied, "Your father, Wunchènewànk, Spirit of the West, once gave you a pipe, symbolizing the peace that came between you two after a settling of your differences. Make such a pipe for the Lenapé that they too through its power might come to find the same peace and understanding, and instruct them in its power and use."

Shortly thereafter, one beautiful day, the great and wise Nanapush was seen standing upon the top of a high mountain, sending up signals of smoke, calling all of his Lenapé grandchildren, our ancestors, to Council. After they were all gathered together in one great assembly in the valley below, Nanapush, the great and gifted being, broke off a piece of stone at his feet and he fashioned the first pipe that was ever seen by our Lenape'wàk. When it was finished, he filled the bowl with the leaves which he pulled off a certain plant, smudged the pipe with *winke'màsk* (sweetgrass), and he blessed it. Then he made a fire of cedar logs and he named it, Tinde Wulankuntowa'kàn— the Fire of Peace. And from this sacred fire he lit this pipe, and he smoked it before all of the people. While he smoked the pipe, he talked with them, instructing them in the meaning and use of the pipe. As he smoked, a great peace, a great feeling of understanding, fell upon them. Indeed, their hearts became filled with a new kind of joy, good feelings and comfort. So, Nanapush, the strong and wise one, gave his Lenapé grandchildren that pipe as a gift, and he told them that the Creator had instructed them to go to a certain place where they would find a sacred plant growing there which they should smoke in the pipe. This plant was the sacred tobacco, which we call *ksha'te*.

So it was that the Creator, through Nanapush, gave four sacred gifts to the people: Tinde Wulankuntowa'kàn, the Fire of Peace; *hupa'kàn*, the pipe; *ksha'te*, the sacred tobacco; and *winke'màsk*, sweetgrass. Nanapush said, "My grandchildren, my Lenapé people, you are given these four gifts, that through their use you might send your thoughts and prayers to Kishelamàkânk, the Creator, and he will hear. Whenever you are in great trouble or need, whenever you are in Council, build such a fire, bring a pipe into your midst, and the spiritual power of the pipe will immediately begin to cleanse your eyes, throats, hearts, minds and Spirits, of all trouble and evil. As the smoke from the pipe rises to the sky, your thoughts and prayers will be heard by the Creator. Peace and order, and good thinking will be restored among the people.

And so it was, from that day long ago, when Nanapush, the

sacred and gifted being, Grandfather of men and every living being, stood upon the top of the Great Mountain and lit the first pipe from the Fire of Peace, that the pipe has been held as sacred and holy, upheld and respected among the people, at all times and all places. So ends the story of the coming of the pipe to the Lenapé people.

HOW MEDICINE BEGAN

At first, long ago, men and women lived to be very old. Some were said to have lived two and three hundred years. Our Lenape'wàk knew happiness and good health.

Then, one day, a mysterious sickness came upon our people, and everyone who became sick died. It seemed as if soon no one would be left alive.

Now, one who had died from the sickness was a young boy. As he traveled along Pimikishika'tèk, the Path of Souls, he eventually came before Nutemahuma, the Keeper Grandmother, who watches over the entrance to the Land of Spirits, and the young boy was sobbing in great sorrow. Keeper Grandmother asked him why he grieved so, and the young boy replied that his people were dying and that he wished for them to be given life.

So, Nutemahuma told the Creator about the young boy, and having pity on the boy and our Lenape'wàk, he decided to send Nanapush to teach them medicine and healing.

Now, Nanapush came, and he was instructed by the Creator to restore the young boy to life. So, he made a lodge and covered it, then he made a fire and gathered twelve rocks, heating them until they were red hot. Nanapush put the young boy's body into the lodge and then brought in the red hot rocks and closed the door. The rocks were glowing brightly in the darkness and now Nanapush poured water on them, creating much steam, and invoking the Creator and the Spirits to help him. The rocks were the boy's body, the fire his inner fire, the water his blood, and the steam his breath. With Spirit came life, and Keeper Grandmother sent his Spirit back into his body; the boy was alive once again, restored, whole and healthy!

Now, in remembrance of this, as a symbol of the sacredness, and the fragility of life, that the people might be reminded of this and that they might hold the gift of life close to their hearts and not take it for granted, the Creator set strawberries upon the Earth. The red of the strawberry is the red of blood, which is life, and all life, like the strawberry, grows to maturity, gives forth seed and new life, and then is gone. However, even though death touches all life in winter, the strawberry leaves are green there under the snow, a symbol of the Creator's promise of the continuation of life even after death. The leaves of the strawberry were given in threes, representing birth, life, and death; also, the three clans of our Lenape'wàk, the Wolf, Turtle and Turkey. As long as we remember clan and family, and the ways of our ancestors, like the strawberry we too shall live through the coming winters.

So, the young boy, being given new life, was given a new name, Wàte'him, "Strawberry." Nanapush gave him a naming ceremony to honor and bless him before the Creator and all of creation.

Wàte'him, having experienced the mystery of life and death, had been given special gifts and a special purpose. The Creator had instructed Nanapush to teach this boy the way of medicine and healing, and so he did. First, Nanapush taught him about the sweatlodge, original instructions from the Creator, the meanings in its construction and ceremony, and how to use it for purification and healing. However, Nanapush knew that it would require more than just the sweatlodge alone to bring health back to the people. So, they fasted and prayed for guidance in vision to help the Lenapé grandchildren from the ravages of the dread sickness which was upon them.

Nanapush was given vision, and in his vision he saw an otter, *kùna'moxk*, in the water. It was sick and had a plant in its mouth. Then some large waves washed over the otter and it disappeared. The water became still and the otter reappeared, with the plant still in its mouth, looking strong and healthy. He was cured. Nanapush woke from his vision and he took Wàte'him into the forest with him. Going to a certain place and looking for the plant he had seen in his vision, he soon found it. The plant was *sukaxkuk chipik*, the black snake root, and the two dug some up to take back with them.

THE GRANDFATHERS SPEAK

Wàte'him and Nanapush built a sweatlodge, *pimâ'kàn*, and they prepared by fasting. In gratitude for the vision and the gift of healing it would bring through the snake root, Nanapush said a prayer of thanksgiving. Together they prepared medicine from the roots and gave it to the people who came to the sweatlodge. All who were sick and who took of the medicine grew well again.

Over a long period of time Nanapush taught Wàte'him. Plants, he was taught, possessed two powers, the power to heal and the power to grow, and that they could give of their powers to other beings. Now, the animals already knew this wisdom, and Wàte'him was told he must learn from them. So, he watched the animals and discovered what plants and which parts of them the animals ate when they were sick or hurt.

He came to know that the power to heal was not a gift given to every person, that it was a gift given through vision. Even for one given such a gift, it was necessary to be careful that one fast and purify oneself to keep this power and to make it grow.

Sickness is part of life, and just as night follows day, so will people get sick and get well. So, Wàte'him was told to teach others and to share his knowledge, so that sickness could be overcome, and the people would know healing and well-being.

Wàte'him, the first medicine man, then chose a young man who had special gifts and vision. The training was long and hard, but such is the way medicine men and women receive their training, one from the other through years of experience.

So eventually Nanapush left, his purpose completed, knowing that the medicine would continue, bringing health and well-being to our Lenapé people.

MOTHER CORN
(KAHESANA XASKWIM)

Long ago, the Corn Spirit, whom we call Kahesana Xaskwim, Mother Corn, left the Earth. She was angry because some young men had said that they did not believe she existed and that the people could never lose their corn seed.

So it was that all of the corn seeds took flight as if they had wings like little bugs. Everyone's corn was disappearing like this, and soon almost none was to be found anywhere. One man was determined that his wife's seed corn would never get away, so he put it in a deer-skin bag and kept it under his head while he slept; but it too flew away in the form of bugs when the bag was opened.

Now, the corn being gone, people were quarreling and treating each other badly due to a lack of food and all of the worries about the coming winter. Finally the winter came and a deep snow fell which covered even the trees. When the Chiefs saw this they said, "The Creator has sent this to punish us," and they cried and grieved for their people so, that the Creator had pity on them and sent a south wind, which melted the snow away.

One day an old man came from the south who said, "The Creator has sent me to help you through your troubles from the snow. Now, my grandchildren, I will give you this thing," presenting them with *sisawin*, an oyster, "to put on the top of your pipe and to give sustanance to your little children. Strike the ice with your pipe and you will be given plenty to eat." So, they fastened the oyster to their pipe and went and struck the ice with it. Every time they did this, an oyster would appear on the pipe. They made a bag to put them in and soon had filled it with oysters and carried them to their village, where they emptied them into a special house, hanging them up to dry. It wasn't long before they had enough to supply the village for some time.

In the morning the old man took a young boy by the hand and told him, "Come, let us go into the middle of the sea and find the Corn Woman. I have come from the Spirit world, to instruct and assist your people." Then away they both went to the sea. After traveling some time on the ice, they came to a hole and the old man took the child by the hand and went down into it. When they got through there was no water, but they saw land all around. The land appeared to be a cornfield, but no corn remained.

Off in the distance they saw a house. The old man said, "That must be the home of the Corn Woman. We shall visit her, but first we shall eat." So they took some oysters out of the old man's pouch and roasted them over a fire. After a while, the oysters opened up as they cooked, and a woman came from the house to their fire. The woman asked the old man if he would give her some of their food as she was so very hungry and it smelled so good and sweet. So he gave her some of the oysters, saying, "Are you the Corn Woman who is called Kahesana Xaskwim, Mother Corn, in the land up above?" "Yes, I am Mother Corn, old man. Why do you ask?" said she. The old man said, "I have come to ask you for some seed corn, to bring it back upon the Earth, for the people are hungry and suffering. I gave some people a medicine to get oysters, but a person can get tired of oysters real quick if that's all there is to eat!"

Then the old man said, "Now that we have eaten we will offer tobacco in thanks to the Creator for this gift of food. Also, we would like to sing and dance for you, Corn Woman!" So, the old man sang and the young boy danced, and Mother Corn was so well pleased with the oysters and the singing and the dancing that her sorrow disappeared, as if a great weight had been lifted from her heart.

"But why should I let the corn be brought back to the Earth among those who are not thankful for my gift of corn and who take me for granted?" asked the Corn Woman. The little boy pleaded with her, crying, "The people of my village would be very thankful if you would give us some corn to take back to them. Many of the people on the Earth are starving, many of them small children such as myself." Mother Corn could not resist the pain of so small a child and her heart went out to him.

In the meantime the old man made her some earrings out of the oyster shells. Corn Woman was touched by this gift. She put them in her ears, and they looked so lovely, she was happy and she cried. But it was not tears that flowed from her eyes when she cried. It was corn seed! Corn Woman said, "From this I will give you each a handful of seed corn to take back with you, and I will teach you special songs and dances. When I hear these songs being sung and see the dances being danced, it will make me very happy. I will know that you are very thankful and I will give you an abundance of corn and crops so that the people won't hunger." The old man and the boy each received a handful of corn seed, gave Corn Woman much thanks and back they went to the land above.

When they came out of the hole in the ice, the old man took the child by the hand and traveled on very fast, as the ice and snow were fast melting away. When they got to the village, the old man said, "Be thankful and glad that we have returned. The corn that has been so long lost is now returned to you. It appeared to me as a woman and she said that you will all be well. She gave us these two handfuls of seed corn which I now give to you." When the people heard this they were overjoyed! From those two handfuls of seed corn came all of the corn which we have now.

The next day some people digging in the snow found a great many wild potatoes, and the woods abounded in deer and game. The Spirit woman had spoken true! The people were very happy in finding such as unexpected abundance of food, and said, "We will now make an offering to our Mother Corn who has given these gifts to us!" So they offered her tobacco. They sang the songs and danced the dances she had taught the old man and the boy. The women went and planted the seed corn, and the corn that they harvested was four times as large as usual!

After the corn ceremony in honor of Mother Corn, the old

man told the people that it was their duty to hold such ceremonies in thanks for the many gifts given to them by the Creator. He told them that the hard times they had just experienced were a punishment for the wrongs they did to each other, and for their lack of faith and thankfulness, and that from this experience he hoped they would learn to be humble, to realize the dependence that they had on all things for their very existence. It is not wise to take the corn and such gifts for granted.

So, we should always thank Mother Corn for a bountiful harvest, and pray that we have one just as good next year, and that we all will enjoy good health. Mother Corn, the Corn Woman, since that time long ago has been held to be very close and dear to our Lenapé people.

THE MASKED BEING
(MISINKHÂLIKÀN)

Long ago, there were three boys who were not treated very well. In fact, their parents did not seem to care whether they lived or died. One day, they were out in the forest thinking about their troubles when they saw a strange-looking hairy person with a large face painted half black and half red. This person said, "I am Misinkhâlikàn, I have taken pity on you and I will give you strength so that nothing can ever hurt you again. Come with me and I shall show you my country!"

He took the boys into the sky to the place where he came from. It was a great range of mountains up in the sky reaching from north to south. While he was showing the boys his country, he promised that they would become stout and strong and should gain the power to get anything they wished. Then he brought the boys back to the Earth again.

In later years, when the boys had grown up and were hunting, they used to see Misinkhâlikàn occasionally, riding on a buck, herding the deer together, and giving his peculiar call, "Ho-ho-ho!"

And so it was that there were three men in the tribe who knew that Misinkhâlikàn existed, because they had seen him with their own eyes.

Now, the Lenapé had always used a bark long house to worship in, but in the earliest days it had no faces carved upon the posts inside. In this house we used to sing about our dreams and visions, but some time after the three boys had talked with Misinkhâlikàn, the people gave up their worship and for ten years they had none.

A great earthquake came then which lasted for twelve moons

and gave much trouble to the Lenapé ancestors. In one of their town a Sakimâ, a Chief, had a large bark house, and there the people met to worship, hoping to stop the earthquakes. Then, they built a new house for this, and when it was finished, they worshipped there, and sang and prayed all winter for relief.

Just after springtime came, they were holding a meeting one night when they heard something making a noise in the forest, "Ho-ho-ho!" in the east. The Chief called for someone to go and see what it was. The three men recognized the call of Misinkhâlikàn and offered to go because they knew who was making that noise and they wanted to find out what he wanted.

So, they went outside and found Misinkhâlikàn in the woods, and asked him what he wanted. "Go back and tell the others to stop holding meetings and to attend to their crops," he answered, "Do not meet again until the fall, when I shall come and live with you. Then I will give your people help through a new ceremony, Xinkwikàn, the Big House. You must carve a mask of wood to look like my face, painted half black and half red, as mine is, and I shall put my power into it, so it will do as you ask. When the man who takes my part puts the mask on, I shall be there with you, and in this way I shall live among you. The man must carry a *taxoxi kowàni'kàn*, a turtle-shell rattle, a bag and a staff just as I do now."

Misinkhâlikàn told them to carve twelve faces on the posts of the Big House and faces on the drumsticks to be used in the ceremony. Then he said, "You must also give me hominy every year in the spring. I take care of the deer and other game animals. That is what I am for. Wherever you build a Big House, I shall keep the deer close by so that you can get them."

"Never give up the Xinkwikàn, for if you do, there will be more earthquakes or other things just as bad."

The earthquakes stopped, and the Lenapé kept the Xinkwikàn and the mask ever after.

* * * * * * * * * * * *

However, in 1924, the last Big House ceremony was held. This was due to cultural changes on the Oklahoma Reservation, whereby the Peyote religion and Christianity were more widely followed. This, coupled with the fact that those who were knowledgeable and capable of performing the ceremony died and people became too few in number to carry it out properly anymore. It is a sad thing for us, but there are many of us today working to bring it back again.

Misinkhâlikàn gave the Big House to our Lenape'wàk, to keep all land and all life in balance and harmony on the Mother Earth. Misink, as we call him for short, is that being which is so well known to everyone today as "Bigfoot" or "Sasquatch." Many people have seen him, many are trying to study and capture him, but none have really listened or believed we Native people when we have talked about him. To we Lenapé, he is a Spirit Being, guardian of the forest and trees, and keeper of the game animals.

We give tobacco offerings to Misink before going into the woods, before hunting, or to give thanks for his work in Nature and for giving us the meat that we eat, which keeps us from hunger.

Misinkhâlikàn is unusual, in that he often takes on physical form, as a great, hulking, hairy ape-like giant. He travels between his world in the sky, just above this Earth, and the Earth. He can leave tracks, which often end suddenly, with Misink nowhere to be found. One place he is frequently seen is where a lot of logging has taken place and where housing development occurs in wilderness areas. He is often seen near creeks and swamps, where he is often seen to vanish, as water is a portal where he passes between his world and ours. Misink often comes as a warning to human beings, that we are not living in harmony and balance with our fellow creatures and with Mother Earth.

GRANDFATHER THUNDER
(MUXUMSA PETHAKOWE)

Muxumsa Pethakowe, our Grandfather the Thunder, was father of the first people, and the Moon was the first mother. But Maxa'xâk, the evil horned serpent, destroyed the Water Keeper Spirit and loosed the waters upon the Earth and the first people were no more. Since then, the Thunderers, Pethakowe'jàk, have always been on the lookout for Maxa'xâk and other such evil water monsters, and when one appears, the Thunderers shoot their crooked, fiery lightning arrows at them, hoping to avenge the deaths of the first people and to make sure that none of their evil shall disturb the harmony upon the Earth or cause harm to our Lenape'wàk.

Long ago, there was a time when Grandfather Thunder was forgotten among our people, unlike Grandmother Moon who has always been remembered and honored by us. He became bitter and despondent over our neglect and forgetfulness of him, and in his anger he came from his home in the west, calling out in a voice that shook the heavens and the Earth. Hidden in clouds he crossed right over the homes and villages of our people. In his fury he shot lightning arrows at the Earth, killing people, burning houses and shattering trees, and the clouds cried their tears of sorrow upon the Earth. Luckily he never stayed in one place too long, and usually was seen traveling towards the east.

At first he would come alone, but after a while his many children came with him, and they frequently brought fear into the hearts of our Lenapé people. Some would come from a cave under the falls known today as Niagara and others came from the mountains where they often made their homes.

At the sight of dark clouds and lightning, and at the sound

70

of the thunder, being the roar of the wings of the Thunderers and the shaking of their rattles filled with bones, which shook the sky, our people became most fearful.

Nanapush finally saw that we, his grandchildren, were in distress and so he came to help us, saying, "You have hurt and insulted your Grandfather Thunder through a lack of respect and thought for him. Grandfathers need to be remembered and honored too, for they also, like grandmothers, have shared in the gift of life and in helping their grandchildren into the future. So, when you first hear Grandfather Thunder in the spring, telling you that winter has ended and that life is again coming to the Earth, burn tobacco and greet your grandfather with prayers. Whenever you hear his voice, do this and you will gain his protection and lightning will not strike you. Grandfather Thunder has charge of the rains that water the Earth and make your crops grow. With the proper respect, he will be thankful, bringing blessings to you, and protect you from the horned snakes and water monsters, and he will come to bring you warnings!"

From that time to this our Grandfather Thunder and our Lenapé people have always been close. We listened to our wise Grandfather Nanapush, and we have always shown respect to Old Thunder and love him dearly, and we always give thanks for his many gifts to all land and life upon Mother Earth.

RAINBOW CROW
(MÀNÀKA'HAS)

Long, long ago, before our Lenapé ancestors walked the Earth,
the weather was always warm and the animals lived in happiness.

Then one day, the Earth suddenly became cold, and white,
sparkling flakes fell from the sky, covering the Earth with its
white softness. The animals, seeing snow for the first time, were
not afraid.

Soon, the snow grew deeper and Axpo'kwès, the Mouse, disappeared. All that could be seen was the tip of his tail, and the
other animals began to get worried.

Then Chèmà'mès, the Rabbit, disappeared. All that could be
seen were the tips of his ears, and by now the animals were
really worried. So the animals met in Council, gathering together in a clearing deep in the forest, to discuss the situation.
They decided that what was needed was for a messenger to
travel up to the home of Kishelamàkânk, the Creator, and ask
him to stop the snow. They asked among themselves, "Who is
willing to make such a journey, to the twelfth heaven, that
distant dwelling place of the Creator?"

Wapink, the Opossum, said, "Kukhus, the Owl, is the wisest.
Perhaps he should be the one to go." "But no," the animals whispered.
"He might get lost in the light of day. So Owl shouldn't go!"

Then Tamakwa, the Beaver, said, "Perhaps Naxànum, the
Raccoon, should go." "No!" the animals argued. "He might
follow his tail instead of his nose. So Raccoon should not go."

Then Shikak, the Skunk, said, "Perhaps Tàme'tut, the Coyote,
should go." "No!" the animals shouted. "Coyote is clever and
loves to play tricks. He might chase the clouds or swallow the
wind. So Coyote should not go."

Then the animals made all kinds of noise. They screeched and howled, hooted and growled, because they couldn't decide who should make the journey to the dwelling place of the Creator and ask him to stop the snow.

In the meantime, the snow got deeper and deeper. The small animals climbed on top of the taller animals so that they wouldn't disappear.

Just as the animals were in their greatest despair, from the top of a tall tree, Mànàka'has, the Rainbow Crow, flew down among them. In the sweetest voice they had ever heard from a bird, Rainbow Crow said, "I will go, I will go!"

The animals were so happy to have a messenger that they sang many songs of praise to him.

Then Rainbow Crow flew high up into the sky, above the snow and the winds, beyond the clouds, the moon and the stars.

For three days he flew, until at last he arrived at the twelfth heaven, the dwelling place of the Creator; but the Creator was too busy to notice him. So Mànàka'has, the Rainbow Crow, began to sing. Upon hearing the singing, the Creator stopped to listen. Never before had he heard such a sweet voice singing or such a beautiful song. Upon seeing Mànàka'has, the Creator said, "Such a gift of song as you have given to me, I now give a gift to you. Tell me what you would choose to have." Rainbow Crow knew that far below, on the Earth, the snow was getting so deep that soon all of the animals would disappear. So he asked Kishelamàkânk, the Creator, to stop the snow.

The Creator replied, "No, Mànàka'has, I cannot stop the snow, for the snow has a Spirit of its own. When the Snow Spirit leaves the clouds to visit with his friend, the Wind Spirit, the snow will stop, but Earth will still be cold."

So Mànàka'has asked the Creator to stop the cold, but the Creator said, "No, Mànàka'has, I cannot stop the cold. All I can do is give you the gift of fire. Fire will keep you warm and will melt the snow so that your friends will be content until warm weather returns."

The Creator picked up a stick, and set it on fire by sticking it into the Sun. Then he handed it to Mànàka'has, saying, "I will give you this gift only once. Now hurry! Fly back to the Earth before the fire goes out!"

Off flew Rainbow Crow.

On the first day, as he was flying down to the Earth, sparks from the fire burnt and darkened his tail feathers.

On the second day, the fire burned brighter and the stick grew shorter, and all of Rainbow Crow's feathers became blackened with soot.

On the third day, the stick of fire was so short, and the fire so hot that smoke and ash blew into his mouth, and his voice became cracked and hoarse. "Caw, caw," he croaked.

Upon returning to the clearing in the forest where Mànàka'has had left the other animals, they were nowhere to be seen. Only the tops of the tallest trees were above the snow. So, Mànàka'has flew down close to the snow, and around and around he went until the fire had melted the snow and his animal friends were safe.

The stick of fire that Rainbow Crow had brought to Earth as a gift from the Creator, became the grandfather of all fires, and for this all the animals gave thanks to him. They danced and sang songs praising Rainbow Crow.

But Mànàka'has flew alone to a distant tree, where he wept. For now he was no longer beautiful, and could no longer sing sweet songs. His rainbow-colored feathers were gone forever.

When the Snow Spirit emptied the clouds and joined the Wind Spirit, the snow stopped. Crow was still weeping. No longer was he Rainbow Crow, but just a plain black Crow. Alas, Crow is what he has been called ever since.

Now Kishelamàkânk, the Creator, heard Crow in his despair and came down from the sky. When he saw Crow, he said, "Soon man will appear on the Earth. He will take the fire and be master of all but you. For being so brave and unselfish, I now give you the gift of freedom. Man will never hurt you, for your meat tastes like fire and smoke. Man will never capture you, for your beautiful voice is now crackly and hoarse. Man will never value your feathers, because your rainbow colors are now black. But your black feathers will shine and reflect all the colors. If you look closely you will see."

RAINBOW CROW

Crow looked, and he saw many tiny rainbows shining in his black feathers, and so he was satisfied.

The Creator returned to his dwelling far above the sky, and Crow returned to his friends in the forest, happy and proud that he was now just a black Crow, with shining feathers full of tiny rainbows.

WHEN THE ANIMALS LEFT
LENAPÉ LAND

Long ago, there was a time when the animals disappeared from Lenape'hokink, Land of the Lenapé. No one could figure out where they had gone. So, finally, the Chiefs sent out the very best of their hunters to see if they could find any animals, but they came back with disturbing news. Not one track had they found! Not one sign had they seen! It seemed as if the animals had completely vanished from our lands!

So, the main source of our food being gone, something had to be done, for winter was approaching and we would surely starve with no meat. So, once again the Chiefs sent out groups of the best hunters to travel over the Turtle Island to look for the animals. Owl assisted them in this search too, for he needed the mice for food. Owl went far to the north to a place of spruce trees, and he saw many animals apparently imprisoned in an enclosure of trees; but they looked content and not the least bit ill at ease.

Seeing that something was strange here, Owl flew down to a low branch and talked to the animals. No sooner had Owl sat on the branch that he was attacked by fierce Giants and their friends, the Crows. Luckily night was falling and Owl was able to escape, and he left as fast as he could fly.

Flying back to Lenape'hokink he reported to the people on what he had seen. So, the Lenapé Chiefs gathered together a large body of warriors to rescue the imprisoned animals, and Owl guided them.

When the warriors arrived at the place where the animals were imprisoned, they were immediately attacked by large numbers of fierce crows. Never had the warriors seen so many! Then they were set upon by the Giants, who came after them with small trees and threw large rocks upon them! The battle that followed lasted for days, with neither side gaining victory. To the warriors something did not seem right, because at no time did the animals try to escape, but just looked curiously upon the battle raging all around them.

Finally, the Lenapé warriors being discouraged, they asked the Giants for a truce. Their adversaries granted the request, welcoming the rest themselves. The Lenapé War Chief asked the animals, "Why is it that you seem unconcerned with our attempts to release you from your imprisonment? We have undergone much hardship and even death for you, but you don't seem to care!"

The Chief of the animals, a large elk, came forward, saying, "You think we are here against our wishes, but this is not so! We wish to remain here and we are content. The Giants have treated us better than you ever did when we lived in your lands!"

Amazed, the War Chief asked, "How is it that we have offended you?"

The Chief Elk replied, "You have wasted our flesh; desecrated our forest homes, and our bones; you have dishonored us and yourselves. We can live without you, but you cannot live without us!"

"How can we make right our wrongs to you? How shall we atone for your grief? Tell us!" cried the War Chief.

The Chief Elk spoke again. "Honor and respect our lives, our beings, in life and death. Do what you have failed to do before. Stop doing that which offends our Spirits."

The War Chief promised, and so the Giants released the animals and they followed the Lenapé back to their homeland. Ever since that time we Lenapé have always offered tobacco and shown the utmost respect when hunting or upon killing an animal for food. We never took more than we needed, and we used as much of the animal's remains as we could.

WÈHIXAMU'KÈS

Once there lived a man of our Lenape'wàk named Wèhixamu'kès, who was regarded by the people in his village as lazy and good for nothing.

One day the men of his village struck up the warpath against their enemies. Wèhixamu'kès wanted to go along, but the others knew that he was liable to lay down and go to sleep just when they needed him most. But although the warriors didn't really like the idea of Wèhixamu'kès going with them, they needed all of the help they could get; so they relented and let him join them. Soon, however, they saw that they had made a mistake. He slept so long the next morning that they had to leave him behind — however hard they tried they could not wake him.

When Wèhixamu'kès finally woke up he found that he was all alone, but he eventually caught up with the rest of the warriors and they made camp. Instead of helping the others, Wèhixamu'kès lay right down again and went to sleep. Again, the next morning when the warriors woke up they tried to rouse him, but they couldn't wake him. So, they ate breakfast and left him behind. They said, "Just let him sleep. Just let him stay there. Let's go!"

Again, Wèhixamu'kès woke up to find himself alone and left behind, but he eventually caught up with the rest. The next morning, to everyone's surprise, Wèhixamu'kès was up early!

So the warriors left camp and traveled till they came to some prairie land, and while going through this they ran into a large number of the enemy, who were too many to defeat. So the War Chief said, "We'll hide in the tall grass and after they pass us by we can go on." So Wèhixamu'kès squatted down as far as he could, but every now and then he would stick his head out. "Look out! The enemy will see you!" the others warned him. But he just couldn't stand it when the enemy passed close by him, so finally he jumped up, yelling a war cry and saying, "Here we are, and we're a large number of warriors!" So the others jumped up and snuck off, not wishing to get caught up in his foolishness. They told him, "Now that you have attracted the attention of the enemy we will leave you to have your way. You can fight them all!" Wèhixamu'kès replied, "All right," but he thought fighting the enemy meant wrestling and hand to hand combat. When the War Chief realized the mistake, he told Wèhixamu'kès, "That isn't what I meant at all! I meant for you to kill them all because they're planning to kill all of us!"

Wèhixamu'kès cried, "Well, why didn't you say so in the first place!?", and he grabbed his ax and went right after the enemy until he had killed every one of them but one. So, Wèhixamu'kès took a knife and cut the ears off this man, just leaving little pieces hanging there, and then he cut his nose off, saying, "Now you will look like an enemy even among your own people. They will be afraid to look upon you. Tell them that I have done this, and if they choose to war against my people, they too will end up looking like this!"

Now Wèhixamu'kès and the other Lenapé warriors headed for a place of great forests. They were hungry but they had nothing to eat. So the War Chief said to the rest, "We should hunt bear so we will have plenty to eat. Now let's scatter about and look for a nice hole that looks like a home. If any of you find this, you whoop, and we'll get the bear together." So they all scattered out through the forest. Soon Wèhixamu'kès was heard hollering off in the distance, just whooping it up! The warriors went running as fast as they could. Wèhixamu'kès had discovered a hole in a tree, made by a bird that lived there. When the warriors arrived, Wèhixamu'kès said, "Here's a hole! It looks as if something is living in there!" The warriors said, "My goodness! Not that small a hole! No bear could live in there!" Wèhixamu'kès said, "Why didn't you tell me to look for a large hole?"

So they all left and kept on looking. Soon someone was heard whooping, but it wasn't Wèhixamu'kès. The War Chief said, "It's a great big tree. There's sure to be a bear in there! Is there anyone who can go up and make the bear come out of the tree?" In those days there was always somebody who could knock on a tree and say, "Come out," and the bear would always come. The War Chief thought that someone would do it in the usual way. Wèhixamu'kès said, "Why, I can do that," and he climbed the tree and crawled into the big hole. He went down after the bear, and told the bear, "Get out of here!", and the bear came out! The warriors then killed the bear, which gave them plenty of food for a while.

They went to a place where there was a lot of wood and set up a camp. Then they skinned the bear and cooked it over a large fire. One of the warriors made a pan of bark, and he had a bucket. He ran the bear grease into the bucket and then poured it into the bark pan to cool. The warriors were camped here for several days.

One of the old men said, "Tomorrow we'll get a turkey and dip him in this grease." So the next morning they all went out in search of turkeys. Wèhixamu'kès went along also, and he soon came upon a flock of turkeys. Now he assumed that the goal was to catch the turkey alive. After much effort he finally succeeded in doing this, and he took it back to camp. When he arrived no one was around, he was all by himself. The old man had spoken of dipping the turkey into the grease, so he thought he would start with the work. After Wèhixamu'kès finished dipping the turkey in the grease, he let him go, and after a while he caught the turkey and dipped him in the grease once again. He kept this up for a long time as the hunters were a long while in returning. By now the turkey was soaked with grease. Then Wèhixamu'kès saw one of the warriors coming. He had just finished dunking the turkey in the grease for the umpteenth time, and the turkey was half drowned. So Wèhixamu'kès told the warrior, "Look, I've got a turkey! I've done just what was said, and I'm pretty tired as I've been dunking this turkey in this grease so long. I think you'd better help me!" The warrior said, "My goodness! You've wasted all of that good bear grease!" The turkey had been kicking and had scattered grease everywhere. "What a mess! That isn't what was meant by dipping turkeys in grease!! First you clean a turkey up good, and then you cook it. Then after it's cooked you dip the meat into the

grease and eat it." Wèhixamu'kès said, "Well, why didn't you
say so!? If I'd have known that I would have had this turkey
cooked long ago!"

By the time the others came back the turkey was cooked and
the warrior told the others what Wèhixamu'kès had done. The
War Chief said to the warriors, "I am going to tell you. Here-
after we must not joke, we must talk plainly or Wèhixamu'kès
might do us harm."

Soon they broke camp and went traveling about. The War
Chief said, "We ought to hunt some deer and take some home."
So, Wèhixamu'kès hunted for several days, but killed nothing.
Finally, he came upon a big deer and killed it. Now, he had
heard the others say that they would take the deer home, but
they didn't mean that when each man killed a deer he was to
go home. It was intended that when many deer were killed,
that all the warriors would return home together. So, when
Wèhixamu'kès killed his deer he skinned the deer legs half way
up so he could tie the legs together with deer skin. He crawled
under and the deer was fastened on him. He had traveled a
long way, when he heard someone whoop. He looked around,
and seeing a large number of men he said, "Goodness! There
are a great many of the enemy!" He didn't stop, but tried to
escape them. However, the enemy soon had him surrounded,
and they said, "Well, we've got you now!" Wèhixamu'kès said,
"Yes, you've got me now, I guess." Ahead of him were steep
rock cliffs, with a thousand foot drop to the bottom; he went
over near them. The enemy warriors crowded around him,
meaning to push him off. Wèhixamu'kès said, "You people must
be very anxious to go down there, so I'll put you there." He
took the deer off his back and laid it down. The enemy warriors soon discovered that Wèhixamu'kès was a man of power.
They tried to get away but they couldn't. They got really weak,
they would run and he would whoop and they'd fall down.
They tried to get away by crawling on their hands and knees,
but they couldn't. So, Wèhixamu'kès began to grab them and
throw them over the cliff. Finally he had thrown them all over
the cliff except one, who he let live to tell the tale to his people.

Wèhixamu'kès went back to camp, and as he was tired from

throwing all of those warriors over the cliff, he threw the deer down and left it for the others to skin. So they cut the deer up and camped there a few days longer.

The War Chief again told his warriors, "Be careful! This Wèhixamu'kès doesn't get a joke! The very thing you tell him, he'll go and do. He may hurt us some day, so choose your words to him very carefully!"

One day, some of the warriors were jokingly saying, "Let's go on a hunt and kill everything alive that we see, and take it home with us." Wèhixamu'kès said, "All right!" While he was hunting he saw one of his companions up ahead. He thought, "Well, he's still alive. I believe I will get him," and so he killed that man. He cut holes in his legs so he could carry the man on his back. Wèhixamu'kès went on further and saw another one of his companions, and so he killed him too, strung him up, and went on home looking for anything that was alive. When he got back, he threw the two men down in front of the people. "Well, this is all I could find alive," he said. The warriors had talked of killing anything alive; the War Chief said, "Now things have happened, just as I told you they would. So now he's killed two men. I told you to choose your words carefully! You have to explain everything to him fully so that he understands it right."

So all the Chiefs told their people that Wèhixamu'kès had great power and that he could do anything. The Chiefs told them to be very careful in talking to him, that when they told Wèhixamu'kès anything, they had to explain it very clearly to him, so he would understand it right.

At that time Wèhixamu'kès became a very powerful man. So, he decided to leave his village, he went a way off and built a *wikwàm* for himself.

One day, a number of men came and surrounded him. They said, "We've got you now!" Wèhixamu'kès said, "Yes, I guess you have! Come in!" He raised the flap of his *wikwàm*, and they all came in. Pallets were spread down around the fire at the center of the *wikwàm*. "Well, sit down, you men. I'll cook dinner before we go," said Wèhixamu'kès. So he went to work and started dinner; he put some big kettles on the fire, put lots of venison in them and covered it with water so as to make plenty of soup. Finally, when the soup was done cooking, he asked the men, "Where's your Chief?" They thought he was going to feed the Chief first, so they pointed him out to him. Suddenly, Wèhixamu'kès grabbed a kettle and threw the boiling soup right in the Chief's face. He had a big wooden spoon in one hand, and he dipped it in the kettles and hurled the hot soup on the others. So they all ran out of the *wikwàm* as fast as they could. When they were all outside, Wèhixamu'kès grabbed his ax and he whooped at the enemy warriors. All of a sudden they could run no further and they fell on the ground. So he killed them all with his ax except one. He cut off this man's ears, his nose and split his fingers saying, "Go tell your people I'm going to live here all the time and they'd better leave me be or they might end up looking like you!"

One day, Wèhixamu'kès went back to hunt with his people and to visit with them. On his way there he came upon a bark house, but saw no one about, so he went in. He thought somebody might be inside. Upon entering he saw a little boy sitting at the fireplace. This boy was about five or six years old, and he was eating parched corn. Wèhixamu'kès looked at him and said, "You live a hard life! I'll just kill you and put you out of your misery!" So he pulled out his ax, but just as he struck at him, with his ax halfway to the boy's head, the boy disappeared and there was a big flint rock there. Wèhixamu'kès stopped his ax just in time, saying, "I nearly ruined my ax on that rock!" He looked and there sat that boy again. "*Aki!*" said Wèhixamu'kès in surprise. "You must be kind of powerful yourself!?" Wèhixamu'kès asked the boy who his friends were that gave him this power. "The Thunder Beings are my friends," answered the boy. Wèhixamu'kès said, "If the Thunders are your friends, then tell them to shoot that tree over there all to pieces." So, the little boy ran out, whooped and told the Thunders to strike the tree with their lightning arrows. In a very short time it started to thunder and lightning. A lightning arrow came out of the sky, struck that tree and tore it all to pieces! The splinters scattered everywhere and almost hit Wèhixamu'kès, scaring him badly. So he told the little boy,

"Indeed, you are a powerful kind of fellow! Can we not be friends?" The little boy agreed, and Wèhixamu'kès picked him up and walked off with him. Wèhixamu'kès let the boy stay with him, and he raised him to be a man.

One day, Wèhixamu'kès said to the boy, "Let's go clean up the evil around this Earth." So they started off, going north, and east, then west. When they were in the cold country to the northwest, they ran into some big giants. Those giants followed them and whooped at them. The giants greatly humbled Wèhixamu'kès, as they had more power than he did. Every time they whooped and hollered Wèhixamu'kès got weaker, until even his bones ached. Now, this boy, this friend of his, had more power than Wèhixamu'kès, so he helped him. With the boy's help Wèhixamu'kès was able to escape from the giants. The boy said to him, "Let's get out of here. We can't go around the Earth. I see that those giants will kill you!" But Wèhixamu'kès grew jealous of his friend because it could be seen that the boy had more power than he did, and he decided that he would kill his young friend.

So, one day, Wèhixamu'kès cooked dinner while the boy lay down beside the fire and went to sleep. Wèhixamu'kès looked at his friend as he slept. He took out his ax and thought, "I believe I'll kill him right now." So he struck at the boy's head with his ax. The boy rolled over and whooped, and the ax stuck into the ground. Wèhixamu'kès told him, "I just wanted to wake you, because dinner is ready." Then came the boy's turn to cook dinner one day, and as he cooked Wèhixamu'kès fell asleep. The boy thought about what Wèhixamu'kès did to him one time when he was asleep. Wèhixamu'kès was sound asleep, and the boy thought, "I could do the same to him, but he couldn't escape." So he picked up his ax. He decided that he would do the same thing to Wèhixamu'kès, but he wouldn't kill him. So, Wèhixamu'kès was lying there with his long hair spread out; he had on a hat of deer hair and a turkey's beard. The boy thought he would chop off his hat, just missing his head. So, he swung and chopped it right off! Wèhixamu'kès whooped and hollered for quite a while. The boy said, "I only wanted to wake you my friend, because dinner is ready."

WÈHIXAMU'KÈS

Then one day, Wèhixamu'kès and the boy went on the war-path against some enemies. In battles with other Indians, Wèhixamu'kès wouldn't fight in earnest against his enemies. He was looking for the chance to kill his friend, the boy. So, one day when they were fighting, Wèhixamu'kès got a chance to hit the boy from behind with his ax, and he split his head wide open. The boy grabbed his head and put it back together the way it was before it was hit, and he told Wèhixamu'kès, "Well, I guess you've got me. You fooled me, I didn't think you would do this to me! I can kill you right now if I choose to, but I'm not going to. I'm going to let you live by yourself." So, the boy left. He lived only one year, and then died. His head came apart where Wèhixamu'kès split it open.

After his friend died, Wèhixamu'kès never went anywhere by himself, and he stayed with his people in the village. Eventually he married. One day, his sister-in-law went down to the creek, and started to chop down a dead tree. Just as it was about to fall, Wèhixamu'kès walked up. The woman saw him just as he got even with the tree. She said, "Wèhixamu'kès, you are so powerful and can do anything. Let's see you catch this tree as it falls." He said, "Yes, I can catch it," and he threw his hands up. So she chopped the tree and it fell right on him. He held the tree up, but he sank into the earth up to his knees. He kept on sinking until he sank up to his neck. The last words he said to his sister-in-law were these, "My life is ending, and I guess I will have to leave you all. I will come back again in the future when a big war is upon the Earth. Then will I come back to help my Lenapé people, when the whites are treating them badly. I will come back to help them bring back their traditions and lifeways. Whenever a woman gives birth to a baby with the little finger cut off at the joint, that baby boy will be me." As Wèhixamu'kès finished talking he sank into the ground, and was never seen again.

THE SEVEN WISE MEN
(NISHASH CHAK LÈPÂ'CHIK)

Once, long ago, there were seven very wise men among our Lenape'wàk. Because of their great wisdom, they were never left alone by the people, and this became a great burden upon them. They never had any time to themselves, or any peace of mind.

So, they held council late one night on their problem and decided, after much consideration, to get some peace by turning themselves into seven great rocks.

One day, a wise and gifted young man of our people was walking along a hillside when he noticed seven very peculiar rocks. As he stopped to examine them more closely, one of the rocks spoke to him. The young man suddenly realized that he was talking to one of the seven wise men. So, seeing that the boy had discovered their secret, they talked to him for a long time, but they asked him not to reveal this secret to the people. It was good to have some peace at long last, and they wished to keep it this way.

However, the people of the village noticed the young man's many excursions to a certain spot on the hillside, and it wasn't too long before someone followed the boy and saw what was going on. Once again, the seven wise men could have no more peace because so many people came to see them.

So, again they councilled among themselves, and they decided to leave the beautiful valley and find another place where they might rest and have some peace and quiet. They went deep into the forest and took the form of seven lovely cedar trees. However, eventually the people saw the cedar trees, and never had they seen such beautiful trees as these, and they began to wonder.

THE SEVEN WISE MEN

Soon it was found that these trees were the seven wise men. So, once again, the seven wise men decided to go away, to some new place, where people could not reach them.

Now, Kishelamàkânk, the Creator, had been watching over them, and seeing their plight he took pity on them. Taking them into his arms, he placed them high up in the sky, and there they became the seven special stars in the night sky.

At long last, the seven wise men found a safe and permanent haven, where they could not be disturbed or annoyed. Yet, they may be seen by everyone, right to this very day. We know these seven stars as Asiskwàtaja'sàk, the Pleiades.

BALL PLAYER
(TUKHIKÀPAPA'LIT)

Long ago, a family went into the forest to hunt, the father, the mother, and their six sons. They found a place where game was plentiful and they made their camp there. The mother built some drying racks to put the meat on, and the older boys starte hunting.

Now the youngest boy never went hunting, but played with his ball all day. For this reason they called him Tukhikàpapa'lit, Ball Player. His ball was a strange one, being the skull of a bobcat. Whenever he hit a tree with it, the ball would stick to the tree; the skull seemed to bite into the tree and stick fast.

They stayed at that camp a long time, going hunting every day and bringing in a great deal of meat, which the mother dried for future use. The boys hunted east, north, and south, but never to the west because their mother had warned them not to hunt in that direction.

But then one day the oldest boy decided that he would hunt to the west despite the warning from his mother. After a while he came to a lake and, looking out upon it, he saw a young woman sitting in the water combing her hair which floated out all around her. He called to her and they talked together a while. Suddenly she disappeared. The boy liked her looks very much and thoughts of her were so much on his mind that he never killed anything while hunting that day. He went home thinking, "I shall try to see that girl again tomorrow," but he didn't tell his mother about what he'd seen.

When daylight came, he again started off to the west. Coming near the lake where he had seen the girl, he began to call upon his dream helper, saying over and over, "Whirlwind, my friend, Whirlwind, my friend." When he reached the edge of the lake, he said, "Whirlwind, my friend, help me to win that girl." He broke a stem of grass which a whirlwind carried right to where the girl was sitting, and through the swirling of the waters it finally returned to the boy, bringing with it a strand of hair from the girl's head. The boy took this home, laying it on the far side of the bed.

Somehow his mother knew what had happened, as mothers seem to do. She said, "*Aki!* Oh dear! my son, I know you have seen that girl!" The younger brother said nothing but kept on playing with his skull ball. When it struck a tree, the skull would bite in and stick.

The next morning the girl came to their camp, bringing a big bowl of bread with her. Everyone, even the mother, was pleased as they had eaten little but meat for a long time.

"I will marry you," she told the oldest boy, "but I am afraid there will be trouble. An ugly old wizard with only one eye and an evil heart, named Red-Feather-on-His-Head, has been after me, but I refused to marry him. Now he is threatening to take me by force, as he has taken several other women already."

The young man quieted her fears, and they were married. Afterwards she found the lock of hair and put it back on her head. She had very pretty, shining black hair.

The hunters brought in plenty of meat and skins, so that the family never wanted for anything, but after a while the parents grew old and tired of living, and departed to the Spirit World.

The youngest boy was growing bigger with the passing of each moon, and he sometimes wandered a long way from camp, playing with his ball and making friends with animals, sometimes not returning until late at night. The oldest brother warned him not to go very far from camp when the hunters were away, but to stay nearby and take care of his sister-in-law.

One morning when the older boys were off hunting, Ball Player forgot what his brother had told him and he wandered away from the camp. Just at that time Red Feather arrived, looking for the girl. As she was all alone, he had no trouble. While he was carrying her off, she kept grabbing hold of the bushes, pulling some up by the roots, but he went on, never realizing that she was marking a trail for her husband to follow.

When the hunters came home that night, they found that the girl was gone. When Tukhikàpapa'lit, Ball Player, came in later that night, he felt very much ashamed that this had happened because he had been forgetful.

In the morning the older brother said, "I am going to look for my wife." Picking up his *api'kân*, his flute, he blew upon it. "If they kill me, within two days blood will flow out of my flute."

In two days the boys looked at the flute.

"*Aki!* Oh dear!" said the second oldest boy. "There is blood on the flute. I shall follow where our brother went." He blew on the *api'kân*. "Look at the flute in two days. If blood flows from it, they have killed me."

"Let me go along, I can bring our sister-in-law back," said Ball Player, but the others did not listen to him. "You are too little," they said.

In two days they looked at the flute, and again there was blood on it. The third brother followed the two that had gone before, refusing the help of Tukhikàpapa'lit, then the fourth brother went, and then the fifth.

The fifth brother followed the trail of the bushes which the girl had pulled as she was being carried away, finally coming to Red Feather's camp. He raised the curtain and entered the *wikwàm*. There sat the wizard and four women, one of them the girl he was seeking.

"Why have you come here?" asked Red Feather.

"I am looking for my brothers who came this way, and my sister-in-law," the fifth brother replied.

"Very well," Red Feather said, and he turned to the girl.

"Cook for this man," he commanded. "He is tired and hungry; he must have come a long way."

The girl broke some bear ribs. After cooking them, she put them in a bowl, which she handed to Red Feather. He held it out to the boy, but when he started to take it, Red Feather snatched it away.

"Do you think I am going to give it to you? I am going to feed it to my *amankaxkti'atmaxkwe*." He untied his fierce, Naked Bear, or Amankaxkwe (short for *amankaxkti'atmaxkwe*), and said, "Amankaxkwe, eat this. When you are through, crush this

boy's skull. He has been talking bad about your sister-in-law."
When the beast had finished the ribs, he attacked the boy and
soon killed him. Dragging the body off, he left it in a ditch.

Two days later, Tukhikàpapa'lit looked at the flute. As he
had expected, there was blood upon it. Now there was nobody
to hold him back. So he went down to the brook where they
got their water, taking with him his father's otter-skin pouch.
Then he whooped and called for his friends. Soon, a lot of
different animals were gathered round, for the boy had been
friends to them all.

"Toad," asked the boy, "What can you do to help me?" Toad
began to breathe hard and every time he puffed, fire came out
of his mouth.

"Ho!" said Ball Player. "That is good enough. You shall be
my pipe." Reaching down, he picked up a snake. "You, Snake,
shall be my pipestem."

He took the otter-skin tobacco pouch and shook it. "What
can you do, Otter?"

"I can bite his spine and break him down!" said Otter.

"That is good enough," said Ball Player. Now he turned to
San'kwe, the Weasel. "What can you do, Weasel?"

"Oh, I can go down his throat and cut his heart off while he
is fighting."

"That is good enough," said Ball Player.

Having enough help now, he climbed up a hill and there he
built a fire. Then he made six arrows and every time he made
one he would throw it in the fire. When it had burned, he
would pick up the ashes and rub them between his hands, and
it would become a good arrow again. Ten times he did this to
each arrow, then he gathered up his skull ball and his other
things and started for the house of Red Feather, following the
trail of bushes which the girl had pulled up.

Eventually he reached the *wikwàm* of Red Feather, and he
walked in.

"What did you come for?" asked Red Feather.

"I am looking for my brothers," said Ball Player.

Red Feather told him, "My Amankaxkwe killed five little boys,
and I threw them out there in the ditch. Maybe it ate your

brothers." Then he turned to the girl saying, "Cook for him, woman. Maybe he is hungry and has come a long way."

While the girl was cooking some bear ribs, Ball Player took out his pipe and tobacco pouch and started to smoke. Every time he drew a puff, the pipe said, "We will kill him!"

"*Aki!*" said Red Feather. "Your pipe sounds bad!"

"That is the natural way for it to sound," replied Ball Player.

Just then Weasel came out of Ball Player's shoulder pocket and climbed all over him. Red Feather saw it. "You have a pretty little pet," he said. "Let us fight our pets. Mine could crush the head off yours in no time."

"Very well," agreed Ball Player. "My pet has never been whipped."

By this time the girl had the bear ribs cooked. Red Feather offered Tukhikàpapa'lit, Ball Player, a bowl of ribs, but he refused.

"I came to look for my brothers, not to eat," he said.

So the Amankaxkwe got the ribs, and Red Feather said to it, "When you are finished eating, crush that weasel's head. The little villain has been talking bad about your sister-in-law."

The Amankaxkwe started to fight, but when it opened its mouth, the weasel disappeared into it. Then the otter-skin pouch came to life and began to chew on the Naked Bear's hind legs. Every time the otter got a mouthful, he would spit it out and go after the legs again until the Amankaxkwe had to sit down to fight. Then the little toad got in front of the Amankaxkwe and began to throw fire at it.

"Call them off," cried Red Feather. "They will kill my pet!"

"No, let them kill one another," answered Ball Player.

Soon the Weasel came out of the mouth of the Amankaxkwe carrying its heart, and the fierce, Naked Bear fell dead.

Then Ball Player set his pets on Red Feather. He threw his skull ball at Red Feather's head, hitting him in his only good eye. There the ball stuck and Red Feather could not get it off. He could not see to fight, so they killed him in no time at all and cut off his head. "You have not really killed him yet. Be careful!" warned the girl.

Ball Player went outside and built a fire, while the women helped him to keep it going by bringing firewood. When it was good and hot and blazing, he threw Red Feather and the Naked Bear on the fire. They burned for a while, then Red Feather's head popped out of the fire to the north. Weasel followed and dragged it back. It popped out four times in all, but Weasel got it every time. The last time it popped out it fell in the grass that grew around the *wikwàm*. Ball Player picked it up and threw it back into the fire and it popped no more.

"Now you have killed him," said the women.

The women all wanted to go with Ball Player, but he would not let them. He took only his sister-in-law. Then they went to where his brothers were lying. He strung his bow and shot one arrow into the air.

"Look out, I might hit you!" he shouted.

When the arrow hit the ground, his oldest brother jumped up, alive and well. This he did for each of his five brothers until all had been brought back to life, whereupon they all went home, taking the wife of the eldest with them.

In this way, it is said, the boy named Tukhikàpapa'lit, Ball Player, conquered the evil wizard, Red-Feather-on-His-Head.

* * * * * * * * * * * *

The Naked Bear, Amankaxkti'atmaxkwe, I believe to have been an actual beast, surviving now only in the folk-memory of my people. It was said to have been immense in size, and one of the most ferocious of animals. Its skin is said to have been bare, except for a tuft of white hair on its back. It attacked and ate people, and the only means of escape from it was to take to the water. It had a keen sense of smell, but its sight was poor.

It could not be killed easily as its heart was small, but the surest way was to break its backbone. However, so dangerous was an encounter with it, that those hunters who went hunting it bade their families and friends farewell, as they were not likely to return.

Mothers used the Naked Bear to frighten their children to be good, threatening them that "the Naked Bear will eat you."

THE LITTLE GRANDFATHER

Once there was a hunter who was returning to his village one evening. As he approached the village, he heard a little singing voice. He tried to find where it was coming from and finally found that the voice was coming from a hole in the ground that was not much bigger than that of a chipmunk.

The hunter said, "Hey, you down in the hole! Who are you?" The singing stopped, and the little voice answered, "I am a Grandfather, a Spirit; if you wish to learn more, give me some tobacco."

So the hunter wrapped some tobacco in a leaf, tied it with a blade of grass and dropped it into the hole.

Soon, the little voice spoke again, "Truly, with tobacco you are stingy. Go and tell your people that I will tell a story to anyone who gives me tobacco or a bit of bread. Now listen to this." Then the little Grandfather told the hunter the best story he had ever heard, then he said, "If you wish to hear another story, don't be stingy with your tobacco." Such was the beginning of stories told for pleasure. Now, this story about stories is ended.

WEMATEKÀN'IS AND THE HUNTER

There once was a man who was out hunting with several friends. They wandered off and left him alone, but even so he was lucky and killed a young buck. He dressed it and put it up on his back, and then went looking for his friends. After searching for a while with no success, he whooped to call them. *"Ju hu!"* he called. Somebody answered, *"O'ho!"* The voice seemed close by, just across the valley. He ran to catch up with the person calling, but when he got there he saw no one. Then he called again, *"Ju hu!"* He heard an answering call, *"O'ho!"*, from the side of the valley he had just left. Every time he crossed the valley, he would hear the voice coming from the place he had just come from.

Eventually the hunter became angry. He threw down the deer and chased the person who was answering him. When he caught him, the hunter found that it was a Wematekàn'is, one of the Little People, carrying a bow with the bark on it. "I'll teach you to answer when I am calling my friends," the angry hunter said. "For that we'll have a fight right here!"

"Ke'hela! Yes indeed!" said the little man. "I'll fight, but wait until I take off my jacket." Wematekàn'is took off a jacket made of cornhusk, and the hunter was ready to fight.

"Wait! let me take this jacket off, too!" said little Wematekàn'is, and he stripped off another one. He kept taking off jackets until he had taken off twelve in all. Each time he took one off, Wematekàn'is became smaller, and by the time the twelfth jacket was off, he was so small that the hunter was ashamed to fight him.

"I won't fight you now," said the hunter. "But I'll give you a name. When you get home, tell your people that someone named you Nox'kumi, Answer-Me. And now I want you to answer me this. Why did you try to fool me?"

Wematekàn'is laughed, "I just wanted to see how strong you were and how far you could run carrying that deer!"

* * * * * * * * * * * *

To we Lenapé, the Wematekàn'is are Earth Spirits (some call them Wood Dwarfs), who live in the forest, often appearing in the form of little people. They help Misinkhâlikàn, the Guardian Spirit of the forests, to take care of the trees, plants and animals.

Wematekàn'is is said to look like a small boy, but he is strong and powerful. Only certain people are able to see him and they usually become noted for their physical strength. Sometimes you may get a glimpse of him in the deep forest as a shadowy something moving out of the corner of your eye, then when you look directly at it to see if something is there, you will see nothing. Wematekàn'is is kind, always helping people, and guides lost hunters out of the woods. If offended, he might ruin a hunter's luck, keep the game away or play practical jokes. Sometimes he even causes illness or takes a person's mind away. We always leave some tobacco for the Wematekàn'is, as this pleases him.

It is said that one day Wematekàn'is was discovered by a little boy who went alone to play in the woods. The little boy came to know him well and liked him very much, going to play with him often. When the other children of the village asked the little boy where he had been, he would say, "I have been to play with my little friend who lives in the woods." Sometimes he could see Wematekàn'is near where the other children were playing and would point to him, but no one could see him.

Very few people see him any more, because of our modern way of living, distant from the Earth and the wildlife. As a result we have lost our connection to the Earth, and people are no longer pure enough to be visited by such supernatural beings.

THE SUGAR MAPLE
(AXSÌNAMÌNSHI)

Long ago, Axsìnamìnshi, the Sugar Maple, was suffering from an intense itching caused by grubs and beetles burrowing beneath his bark. Though he had many arms and fingers, he could not scratch himself. The itching became unbearable, and all that he could do was to writhe in discomfort and torment. He could do nothing by himself to relieve his suffering!

Finally, unable to bear the itching any longer, he called out to the squirrels, porcupines and beavers to help him, but they were concerned only with their own affairs and did not offer any help. All they did was to offer their sympathy.

Next, Sugar Maple called to the birds. They too, felt sorry for him, but could do nothing.

Then, Papa'xès, Woodpecker, came along, and he said he could help. So, he brought his cousins, Ulikwàn, Flicker; and Titàs, the Downy Woodpecker. All of them worked very hard and finally were able to pick up every pest from Sugar Maple's bark, and his itching stopped! What a relief! Axsìnamìnshi thanked Woodpecker and his cousins most happily, and they thanked Sugar Maple for the good meal of grubs and beetles.

Years later, Papa'xès was in distress. Not knowing what to do, he at last came to Axsìnamìnshi, who he hadn't seen in a long time, and he related a sad story to him. Due to a long period without rain, Papa'xès was dying of thirst, and asked Sugar Maple if he might help.

Sugar Maple, remembering the help he had received from Woodpecker, told him, "Go to my trunk and drill some holes and they will fill up with my sap."

Woodpecker flew down and pecked away at the trunk, making

many holes. The holes then filled up with sap, and Woodpecker drank and joyfully slaked his thirst. Woodpeckers have been drinking from trees ever since.

It was from the Woodpecker, that our Lenape'wàk learned that trees give sap and can be tapped.

THE BOY WHO LIVED WITH BEARS

Long ago, it is said, a young boy was lost while playing with some children in the woods. A woman with two children found him and took him to her house, but the boy soon discovered that this woman was really a bear with two cubs and that the house was a great hollow tree trunk.

It was some time before the other children who were playing in the woods with the young boy realized that he was missing. They looked all over for him, but he was nowhere to be found. So, the children went back to the village and told the parents of the young boy. It was evening, but they got some people to help them and they began hunting for him. All night and all the next day they looked for him, but still they did not find him. Finally, after several days, the Chief said, "It is useless to search for him any further, for not even the best trackers can find him. Some wild animals must have killed him, or an evil Manìto, a Spirit, has taken him away."

It was not long after this, while hunting squirrels, that a young man saw some creatures playing around in the woods. Closer and closer he crept to get a better look so he could see what they were. Now, coming closer he saw that it was a small boy and two bear cubs. The young hunter recognized the boy as the one who was recently said to have been lost. So he returned to the village and spread the news of what he had seen.

Now the mother bear knew that soon the people of the village would come to take the boy away from her, and she felt very sad because she had grown to love the young boy as one of her own. She knew too, that when the people came for the boy that they would probably kill her.

Meanwhile, the young hunter was telling the people of the village, "Down there, in the big forest, I saw two bear cubs playing with the young boy who we thought was lost. There is a big tree there and a hollow very high up, a hole up there in the tree. I saw these animals playing, so I crept up to get a closer look, that is how I could see them so well. But they noticed me and ran into the hole in the tree to hide."

The parents of the lost young boy were told what the hunter had seen, and they gathered the men of the village together. Then they all went to the spot in the forest where the young hunter had last seen the boy. The men said, "Now we can expect to be in danger because a female bear with cubs is very fierce when she has young." When the mother bear noticed the men, she at once climbed down from her den in the tree. As she came close to them they shot and killed her. Then one of the men climbed up into the tree and brought down the boy and the little cubs of the mother bear they had killed.

Then they brought the young boy home and they made pets of the little bears. The small boy who was thought to be lost told his story: "I was the cause of that mother bear being killed. She told me that she wanted me to stay with her, to be a part of her family, but that it would be up to me to decide what I wanted to do. She said that if I stayed the people of my village would one day come for me and that she would most likely be killed. Though mother bear wanted me to stay, I should have left. I did not discover that they were bears until after the mother bear and cubs had found me. She must have held some power over me as thay first appeared as a woman and two children. Her death makes me cry, because I was treated well and I could understand what the bears said when they spoke."

From the day that the young boy was brought home they had kept the little bears as pets, until they were full grown. Then it was said, "We have now raised these bears, but we know they are orphans and that it is not right to turn them loose until we have first done a ceremony of pleading. It is our custom that we offer something to the animal and make peace with the bear Spirit before releasing them." So, they put wampum around the necks of each bear, saying, "Now, our relation, the time has come for you to have your freedom. But this boy, your brother, belongs here, and yourselves, Grandfathers, you must return to the forest. And so we offer this wampum to you through this ceremony, as your heart. When you think of us you can say, 'Back there live our relations.' But do not approach us any more, because our hunters may not recognize you and might shoot you. The wampum will take care of you in the future, in case sorrow comes, and shall serve as a guardian of your health. We also, in so giving you this, shall not be overcome by anything evil. Now, once again, Grandfathers, I have said enough in the way of friendship. *Wanishi!* Thank you! Go now!"

THE STUBBORN GIRL

Long ago, when the Lenapé lived in the east, we were many then. There it is said was a girl who was very, very stubborn, and everyone in her village knew this.

One evening, in autumn, as all the villagers were warming themselves by their fires, a dog suddenly appeared. He was wet and shaking from the cold. The stubborn girl saw him first, and she went over to the dog and pushed him over. She said to him, "Tell a story! Tell a story! Probably you know many things."

The girl's mother said, "Leave that dog alone!" But the girl was so stubborn that she pretended not to hear her mother, and she again went up to the dog and pushed him over. Again, she said to him, "Tell a story!"

Finally the dog sat down. He said, "Yes, I will tell you a story. In three days time you will be lying under red dirt."

At this the girl got very scared, and her mother went and told everyone in the village, and their Chief.

The dog spoke the truth, because three days later the girl disappeared. She was nowhere to be found.

This admonition, kept alive by tradition even to this day, comes from this incident: the old people say, "A person should not question or abuse dogs. Before a person comes to where Kishelamàkâng, the Creator, lives, when they leave this Earth, they will first have to cross a huge bridge. All the departed dogs guard this bridge. The bridge is at a fork in the road on the Milky Way in the sky. All of the Lenapé who live well walk the road beyond the bridge guarded by dogs. Those who live badly walk the other road, never stopping. That's why it is trodden down. No one who has done harm to a dog will be allowed to cross over to the other side."

THE GREEDY MAIDEN

Once, long ago, before the Wapsini, White Man, came to our land, there was a Lenapé maiden upon whom Kishelamàkânk, the Creator, wished to give a blessing of faith and understanding.

The Creator led the maiden to the edge of a large field of *pawim*, white corn, which was so large that as far as one could see, the valley was covered with blossoming corn, and all the cornstalks were gently swaying to the singing of the wind. Indeed, it was a lovely and wonderful sight for her to see. And while she was standing there, a Spirit voice spoke to her, saying:

"Young maiden, you are now becoming a woman, and in the field before you are many ears of corn. Listen well to my advice. Those who pick good ears of corn are those who pluck them with faith, and with an honest heart. In doing this they shall enjoy the blessing of the medicine and Spirit of the corn, and that blessing shall be only as great as the size and beauty of the ear of corn that was chosen.

"Young maiden, you shall pass through the field but once, and pluck for yourself one ear of corn, and you must take it as you are walking forward. Be alert. Be cautious. Be very careful! Pick an ear of corn that is full and fair, and according to its size and beauty so shall be its value to you as good medicine for the rest of your life."

The young maiden offered her thanks to the Spirit voice, and then set forth on her quest. As she walked along, she saw many ears of corn, large, beautiful, ripe and good. Careful judgement should have shown her that any one of them would possess a virtue that was good enough, but greed and selfish desire came forth in her eagerness to grasp the very best. So she left the unblemished ears of corn behind, hoping and craving for one still better.

THE GRANDFATHERS SPEAK

The daylight passed by very rapidly, soon the deepening shadows began to dim the dying day, and now she reached that part of the field where the corn stalks were shorter, and the ears of corn much smaller, and here the choice was less and poorer. Regretfully, she now remembered the many good and sound ears of corn that she had left behind. But her wounded pride would not let her pick from the poor corn that was now everywhere around her. Here she saw not one ear of corn that bore perfect grain. So, the maiden went on seeking, hoping and searching. Alas, to her great sorrow and disappointment, she found the cornstalks grew ever more feeble, blighted and useless.

At long last, after suffering much despair, all of the surrounding field began to disappear into the fast approaching darkness, and now she found herself at the edge of the cornfield without having plucked even one ear of corn. There was no need for the voice of the Spirit to rebuke her, everything became very clear to her now, but it was too late!

However, the young maiden did not flee like a whimpering coyote into the night. Instead, she gathered up her courage and returned to her village. Upon arriving there she made a great campfire near her *wikwàm*, and she gathered her best and dearest friends around the fire, and while the flames crackled and leaped forth towards the starlit sky, while a wolf howled in the forest, while the crescent moon hid behind a passing cloud, she told her friends all about her grievous adventure, and she warned them not to follow in her footsteps. Then, very sadly, very regretfully, she bade her friends goodnight. Next morning her elm bark *wikwàm* was empty. Her canoe was gone, and from that day onwards, no one has ever found out where she went on that fateful night. All she left behind was this story.

THE PRETTY MAIDEN

There once was a young woman who was very pretty. All the young men greatly admired her and wished her for their wife, but the young woman spurned all of their advances and would have no suitor.

Seeing this, the animals, Tamakwa (Beaver), Shikak (Skunk), and Kukhus (Owl), held council about the pretty maiden. They said to each other, "I sure would like to have this woman for my wife."

Owl said, "If we try really hard, one of us will surely have this woman for a wife!"

"Owl, you go first and see this woman. Maybe she will desire to be your wife!" said Beaver and Skunk.

So Owl went to see the young woman. He asked her, "Would you come with me and be my wife?"

"You are far too ugly! I wouldn't have you! You have big eyes! No, I wouldn't have you for a husband!" replied the young woman.

So, his feelings hurt, Owl went sadly back to Beaver and Skunk. "That young woman wouldn't have me!" said Owl.

Next, Skunk went to see the pretty young woman. Upon meeting her, Skunk said, "Would you come with me and be my wife?"

"I wouldn't have you! You are way too ugly, and you stink! No, I wouldn't have you for a husband!" said the young woman.

So, Skunk went sadly back to the others, his self-esteem in tatters. "I, also, could not get this woman to be my wife!" bemoaned Skunk to Owl and Beaver.

Skunk and Owl talked it over and agreed, "There is nothing we can do to get this woman to be our wife."

But Beaver had an idea. He said, "I know how I can get that young woman to be my wife! Way over there in the creek where

105

she gets water is a log she stands on, that runs into the creek. Now, if I go and gnaw that log nearly in two, when she goes to fetch water, she will fall into the creek. Then she will send for me so that I can help her. Maybe she will be thankful and choose to be my wife."

So, Beaver went and chewed the log. Next morning when the young woman went to fetch water, she went out onto the log, which broke instantly; the pretty woman fell into the creek!

She cried out, "I wish that Beaver were here, he could swim out and help me!"

Beaver heard her cries for help and he went over to save her. As he came up to her in the water, he asked her, "Will you come and be my wife?" But as with the others he too was insulted.

"I could never have you for a husband. You are ugly, your teeth are too broad and your tail is big and flat like a stirring paddle!" said the young woman.

With that, Beaver broke down in tears, and took off to tell his friends Owl and Skunk. He said, "That young woman has no respect for anyone. She insulted me and made fun of my tail, and she refuses to be my wife!"

In the meantime the pretty young woman was carried away by the current down the creek, and she drowned, because no one would help her.

THE MASTODON
(YAKWAWI)

It was long, long ago, in the most ancient times, when Kishelamàkânk, the Creator, used to appear and talk with our wise men (*lèpâ'chik*) and council with our people. At that time, our people understood the ways of the forest, and the Creator was pleased and very close to his Lenapé children.

At that time, our Lenape'wàk believed that courage, truth, honesty, and generosity were virtues necessary to admit one to Awâsakàme, the Land Beyond. The Lenape'wàk were good and obedient children, following the original instructions given to them by the Creator, and so he was interested in our well being.

It was in that time, long ago, that there were mighty beasts that walked the forests, valleys and plains upon our Mother Earth. Many of these are found no more.

Yakwawi, the Mastodon, was one such beast, placed upon the Earth to be useful to man; but the great monstrous beast was fierce, powerful and invincible. Its hide was so strong and so thick that the sharpest spears and arrows could hardly penetrate it. This terrible creature made war against all the other animals that lived in the woods and on the plains; other animals that the Creator put here to be used as meat for the Lenapé people.

Then one day, a great battle was fought in which all of the animals joined together against the Yakwawi'àk, Mastodons. The Creator told the Lenapé that they were also to take part in this fight, and if necessary they should kill the Yakwawi'àk.

Our Old Ones have told us that the legendary Great Bear also came to help, and that he was seriously wounded in this battle, which is said to have taken place in the Ohio River Valley, west of the Alleghenny mountains.

During the battle, Kishelamàkânk, the Creator, came and sat upon a flat rock on top of the Alleghenny mountains to watch. Great numbers of the giant Yakwawi'àk came and still greater numbers of the other animals.

The battle was fierce, and the slaughter terrible! The mastodons were gaining victory and the Ohio River Valley ran thick with the blood of the fighting animals. But slowly the battlefield turned into a great quagmire, and many of the Yakwawi'àk, because of their great weight, sank into the mire and were drowned. (This is why the land now called Kentucky was called the dark and bloody ground, because of all the blood that was spilled there. It became a common hunting ground for the various tribes, as no one would set up a village there, being greatly afraid of the ghosts of those slain Giants.)

Now, the Creator became very angry with the mastodons, and from the top of the high mountain he hurled bolts of lightning at them until all of them were destroyed, except one very large bull. This bull cast aside the lightning bolts with his tusks and defied everything in his path, killing many of the other animals in his rage, until at last he was badly wounded.

So, he turned and fled, bellowing as he crossed the Ohio River; he ran along the mighty Namès Sipu, the Mississippi River; then he turned and swam the Great Blue Lakes, and he was groaning with pain as he disappeared into the far reaches of the northland where, it is said, his evil Spirit lives to this very day.

Traces of that great battle may yet be seen. The marshes and swamps are still there and in them the bones of the Yakwawi'àk are still found as well as the bones of many other animals. In that great battle there was a terrible loss of animals that were made for food for our Lenape'wàk, and the people were sad at heart to see such a waste of meat and fur.

So, in remembrance of that day, Kishelamàkânk, the Creator, caused the cranberry (*pa'kim*) to grow in the marshland, that it could be used as food by humankind. The coat and covering of the cranberry is the color of blood, in remembrance of that awesome battle that took place in that time long ago.

NO HUNTER AND THE WATER MONSTER
(MÀTÀLÂ'WIT ÂK AMAN'KAMÈK)

Màtàlâ'wit, No Hunter, unlike the other boys in his village, did not like to hunt, and he refused to go with them when they went off hunting. People would tell his grandfather, "That boy is good for nothing."

So one day, his grandfather built a raft and he and Màtàlâ'wit paddled out to an island. "You go hunt birds while I build a fire," his grandfather said. For he was going to trick his grandson into taking care of himself. Grandfather offered tobacco and prayed that the boy would find the wisdom he needed.

"I'm leaving," his grandfather shouted to his grandson across the island, and so he left the boy behind, crying. Màtàlâ'wit cried until the fifth day, when a little skunk interrupted him, saying, "I'll take you home."

"You can't, you're too little," said another voice. "I'll take you home." It was Aman'kamèk, the Water Monster. The little skunk ran away and Màtàlâ'wit cried in fright; this was most unusual, for water monsters chase and drown people, unless the Thunder Beings come to their rescue with their lightning arrows.

"Climb on my back and hold on," said Aman'kamèk to the boy, "and warn me if you see the Thunder Beings coming." They were halfway to shore, when the boy shouted, "Here comes a black cloud!" And he almost fell off, as the water monster suddenly turned back towards the island. They waited one day, and then they tried again. "Hold on tight!" the monster shouted, and he traveled towards shore so fast that the frightened boy thought there would be no need to mention that hundreds of Thunder Beings were rattling their pots of bones and chasing them. But the speed of the monster worked against him, for he crashed and slid way up on the beach, and so he was unable to get back into the water in time to escape them. Pethakowe'jàk, the Thunder Beings, flew off, one carrying the horns, and another carrying the tail of the water monster.

The boy staggered home with an extremely empty stomach and had his lightning burns treated by a medicine man. "The Pethakowe'jàk, Thunder Beings, have given you great power," his grandfather told him later as he ate. "Go to a tree that has been struck by lightning, build a fire and offer tobacco there, then shoot an arrow into a fire-blackened log there," Grandfather told him. So Màtàlâ'wit did as he was told. The log turned into a black bear and the people gathered to share the meat with their powerful new hunter.

THE HUNTERS AND THE TURTLE

Once upon a time, there were twelve men who went out hunting for food for their village. They traveled a long way and had stopped to camp several times, but they could find no game. Then, as they traveled along, they came upon the trail of a large creature. There were huge footprints and flat marks on the ground. They scratched their heads, and asked each other, "What kind of creature could have made such a trail?" They followed the tracks for a long way and finally caught up with the creature. It was a huge, monster turtle! One of the men said, "That turtle is as big as a *wikwàm*!" They were truly amazed, for never had a turtle such as this been seen before!

Then, they all climbed on its back to look it over; they decided to ride on the turtle's back instead of walking. So, they all sat down on the back of the turtle, and it set off. They rode for several days, until they came to a large body of water. There was water as far as the eye could see, and the turtle kept going, heading straight for the water. As the turtle was about to enter the water, the men tried to jump off — but they were stuck fast and couldn't get off! Luckily, one man managed to break free just before the turtle went under. He headed back to the village of his people and told them what had happened: that they had found a monster turtle; that they rode this turtle, and how it headed for the big water; that they tried to jump off, but were stuck fast, and he told them how he had managed to jump off, but how the others went right along into the water on the turtle's back. He said, "The last I saw of the others was their heads disappearing under the water!"

So, the people gathered together in Council, to discuss what the hunter had told them. They did not believe that those men who were carried away by the turtle were dead. Considering the way it happened, there was some mystery about it. Indeed, something unusual was at work. They asked each other, "How can we get our men back from that turtle?"

Now, the Shawnee have always been close to our Lenapé people, since ancient times. A Shawnee man, upon visiting the village, told our people there that he knew of a medicine and a song that went with it, that he thought could be used to call back the turtle and so save the men. This was a powerful medicine for attracting animals and it never failed. So, the Elders, the Shawnee, and the man who had jumped off the turtle's back, went back to the spot where the turtle was last seen, and they camped nearby.

The Shawnee proceeded to make the medicine. He put it into a bowl of bark upon the ground in front of them. They were all sitting in a half circle, facing the water. They were on the north side. They all began to sing the medicine song, calling the monster turtle to return. After they had been singing for a while, all of a sudden they heard a big roar as if some large water-animal were coming. They thought it must be the turtle. But first one kind of water animal appeared, then another, then a crayfish, but no turtle. When the animals came, they would make right for that medicine and stop right in front of it. Then the men would push them back, saying, "We don't want you"; but then another would appear. Next, a big snake came, the largest in the world, and with huge horns on its head! All kinds of lightning, all kinds of colors surrounded them. "Something great is coming this time, maybe this time it's the turtle with the men!" the people said, before they saw that it was the Great Snake. When it got to where the medicine was, it stopped and lay still. The men went up to look this snake over and said it was the prettiest animal they had ever seen. It was decorated with different colors all over its head. They decided to take some of the scales off its body, as such creatures caused the Thunderers to come, and could be used as medicine for making rain. When they had finished getting the scales off, the men spoke to the snake, and told him that they didn't want him either, and they pushed him back into the water.

After the snake had disappeared, once again they heard a

roaring in the water, and the people knew it must be the turtle. They said, "We have had everything else in the water come to this medicine except the turtle. It must be the turtle this time!" The water heaved and bubbled as the creature approached. They saw that it was indeed the turtle — and, amazingly, the men were still on its back and still alive! The turtle came right up to the medicine. The Chiefs then asked a wise old man, "How shall we talk with him and let him know what we want?" The wise old elder said, "We will use tobacco. Kishelamàkânk, the Creator, put tobacco here on this Earth to be used for this purpose, whenever we want anything from animals or Spirits."

So, they gave the turtle some tobacco and tied it around his neck. The old man said, "Here is some tobacco we wish to give you. It is yours, take it along with you when you go. We don't want you, my brother, but only ask that you give our men back to us so they can hunt and get food for our people!"

With these words, the men on the turtle's back woke up as if they had been in a deep sleep. Slowly, they came back to their senses. They saw the daylight and the sun shining. Realizing their situation, they got off that turtle as fast as they could!

"*Wanishi!* Thank you! You may now return to your home, my brother!" the old man said to the turtle, and with that the turtle turned and slid back into the water and was never seen again.

Then a man who had been on the turtle's back said, "Where we came from in the water, everything appeared to be the same as it is here on the Earth, except there was no sun. There were lots of people there, just as there are here, and some animals."

Those men had been gone six months on that turtle's back before they returned!

The old man said, "That was no ordinary turtle! It must have been a great Spirit turtle, and it took you to the World of Spirits below this Earth, that's why there was no sun. You are fortunate to have been able to return!"

So ends this story.

* * * * * * * * * * * *

THE GRANDFATHERS SPEAK

In the early part of this century, the medicine of the snake's scales still existed. They were passed on in a certain family. The scales were put into a split of wood; by putting this in a branch and throwing water on it, it would rain enough to meet the people's needs. These scales were also reputed to give luck in hunting and in trapping. Where this medicine is today I don't know — do you?

THE WOMAN WHO LIVED
WITH SNAKES

Among our ancestors, who lived the old ways, when a girl came into her Moontime (menstrual period), she was sent to live for this time in a special hut on the edge of the village. There she would stay until her time was over. During this time, lasting about ten days, the girl was brought food by the women of her family. She was not allowed to see or talk to any boys or men. At the end of her time, she would receive fresh clothes and a bath. Only then could she return to the village.

It was after one of these times that a young girl was returning to her village. She was wandering down a path when all of a sudden the air turned warm. She saw all kinds of beautiful flowers and the birds were singing cheerful songs. As she bent over to pick a flower, she was startled by a man's voice. She looked up and saw a handsome young man sitting on a fallen log. He wore white buckskin clothes. His moccasins had perfect beadwork and his hair was in long black braids.

The young man asked her where she was going, and she told him that she lived nearby and was returning home. Surprisingly, the young man told her that he already knew where she lived.

She was so ashamed of her clothes that she started to run away; but he ran after her, asking her if she would go with him to his home in the north. He told her that he would like her to meet his mother. The young woman was so in love that she agreed and went home with him.

Soon they came to a peaceful lake. He told her that he lived at the bottom of the lake and that he wished her to be his wife. She looked into his bright black eyes, and her heart melted. So, he took her by the hand and they both walked into the water and soon disappeared. The young girl was frightened at first, but the lake was so pretty. She saw all the fishes and plants that live in the lake. Then they came to a big house in the deepest part of the lake.

The handsome young man opened the door and there stood an old woman. He told the young girl that the woman was his mother and that she would take care of the young girl and show her how to live at the bottom of the lake.

Time went by fast, as the young girl and the old woman were kept busy. She was happy for a while, but soon she began to miss her family.

One day after her husband returned from hunting, he found the girl crying. She told him that she was very lonesome for her family, and wanted to return to her village for a visit. He got very angry with her and told her that she couldn't return to the village, and that his mother would keep a watch on her and make sure she didn't run away. However, he told the young woman that if she got lonely she could walk around in the forest nearby if she wanted. But he warned her, "Be sure there is not a cloud in the sky should you leave the lake! If there are clouds you must not leave!" The young woman listened to him and heeded his words.

She became very sad. Every day she wanted to go home to her village. The old woman told her that when the young girl married the young man, she had left her land and family. If she went back, bad things would happen, she was told.

She loved her husband, but she knew something was wrong. She had been taught that life was not supposed to be sad. Day after day the young girl would cry for her people. She would sing her village songs and long for her family.

Now the old woman grew tired of seeing the young girl so unhappy. So, one morning after her son had gone out hunting and was out of sight, the old woman told the young woman that now would be a good time to escape, and that they must leave right away. She told the woman that her son had fooled her, and that they were really horned snakes, the offspring of Maxa'xâk. So, the young woman followed the old lady for a while, until they came to a river. The old lady said, "We must cross this river to get you to safety. Don't be afraid and climb onto my back." So, she got onto the old woman's back and they began to swim across the river. When they arrived at the river bank and had walked a few steps, the young woman turned around and was at once filled with fright! The old woman had spoken true, for there before the young woman was a snake with horns! Then the young woman heard thunder and noticed the sky was darkening. All of a sudden, there was an awful cracking noise, and she was blinded by a flash of bright light. When she could see again, there lay the horned snake burnt and smoking — it was dead! The woman didn't know what had happened, she was so shocked and confused.

She heard voices, and looking up she thought she glimpsed some flying creatures in the sky, which she knew must be Thunder Beings. The woman called to them and asked why they had killed the snake, and a thundering voice told her that it was their duty to rid the Earth of such evil snakes. The voice then told her to return to her people, and assured her that nothing would harm her along the way, for they would watch over her. So, she left to return to her village. As she was going along, she saw a fire, and someone standing beside it. As she came closer, she saw what looked like a little boy with a big stomach; he was cleaning a turkey.

It was then that she realized that he was a Wematekàn'is, one of the Little People of the forest. When she approached him, he greeted her and told her that he was expecting her. He put some leaves into a pile and invited her to sit down saying, "My Grandfathers, the Thunderers, told me you would be coming and asked that I help you!" He told her he was going to roast the turkey and that she should join him to eat, which she did.

The little man cooked that delicious turkey and after they were through eating, the Wematekàn'is told her, "Now I must doctor you, for I see you are pregnant with snake children. I will try to help you, for if you give birth to them it will surely end your life. Don't be afraid! I will use these two medicine arrows." He shot each of them into her stomach, then pulled them out, one at a time, and she was surprised to see that each one had a small snake on the end of it! The Wematekàn' is then threw the snakes into the fire. He told the woman that she would be all right, and to go home.

So, she returned to her village, and late that night her mother and grandmother spoke with her as she was resting. She told them of her life in the lake. She told them she didn't know that she was living among snake people. Her grandmother said, "That is the way of life. When young girls fall in love they go blind and can't see how a man really is."

Meanwhile, far away, the son of the old snake lady, he returned from his hunting and found his mother dead near the river bank; at once the Thunderers set upon him. He changed into a snake, dived into the river and stayed in his watery home, never more venturing out or trying to fool young women.

THE BIG FISH
(XINKWENA'MÈS)

Once there was an old grandmother whose six-year-old grand-daughter became pregnant. Now, there was no way this could have happened, as the girl was well cared for. Grandmother had kept a careful watch over the young girl, not letting her out of her sight.

Then came the day when the girl was to give birth. So, Grandmother and some women made preparations to deliver the child. But imagine their shock and disbelief when, instead of a baby, the young girl gave birth to a little fish! When Grandmother saw it, she said, "Can this be my grandchild?!" She didn't know what to do! "How could this be?" she asked herself. The fish being a water animal, and Grandmother not knowing what to do with it or how to care for it, she picked it up and took it to a swampy area nearby. "Here it will at least have a chance to live," she said to herself. She put the little fish into a pocket of water there and the little fish swam around and around in a circle.

The next morning, she went back to the swamp to see her grandchild, the little fish. But when she got there she was amazed to see a big lake there. The little fish had grown substantially; but it was still swimming around in a circle!

The lake continued to grow each day, growing to an enormous size; and the fish became the largest anyone had ever seen! The young girl, the mother of the fish, went over there one day to see her fish-child, but she couldn't even see it because the water had become so deep.

Then it happened one day that some people who went over to the lake never came back! No one knew for sure whether the big fish had killed them or not. However, it soon became obvious that anyone who went to the lake never returned, and one day the fish was seen eating someone.

Now there was no doubt that the fish was responsible for all the deaths of the people who had gone to the lake. The Chiefs councilled together to find a way to kill the fish, as the only way to stop the killing. They were sure that there would be someone among them who could find a way to kill it. Some medicine men got together, but they could find no way of getting rid of it, no matter what they did! Then the bravest warriors got together, but try as they might they could not kill the big fish and they almost were killed themselves. Finally, the Chiefs were in despair and at their wits' end, not knowing what to do. In the meantime anyone who ventured close to the lake was never seen or heard from again.

Now, there was a very old woman who lived at the edge of the village with her two grandchildren, two boys. The old woman went to the village Councils every day. One day, one of the grandchildren asked the old woman why she was always going to Council. She explained everything to him, saying, "There's a big lake over there and it grows larger and larger each day, and there's a fish there that grows larger too! He will soon eat up the whole tribe if he isn't stopped!"

"Well," said the boy, "I can kill him!" So, the old woman, knowing that the Chiefs were looking for someone to do this, went to Council next morning. She told the people there that her grandson knew how to kill the big fish, that he had an idea. So the Chiefs sent a messenger to get the boys and bring them to Council.

So the messenger went to collect the boys, and they went with him and appeared before the Chiefs. The Head Chief asked them, "Well, grandchildren, I understand that you can kill that fish over in the big lake?" The little boys said, "Yes, that's what we said we could do." The Chief said, "My little grandchildren, that's why we've been in Council so long, trying to find someone who can kill that big fish. Although we don't see how you boys could kill the fish, if you boys do you shall receive all of these wampum beads, as an expression of our thanks and as a blessing from Spirit for the great deed you would do for your people."

So, they went home with their grandmother; but when night fell they did nothing, just sat around the fireplace. Grandmother wondered how the boys planned to kill the big fish, and she watched them carefully. When bedtime came the little fellows made their beds pretty close to the fireplace, laid down as usual and talked a while. Grandmother lay in bed awake. She didn't want to go to sleep, but was going to watch the boys to see if she couldn't find out their plans. The little boys lay still and silent in bed pretending to be asleep. Soon Grandmother couldn't fight sleep any longer, and she dozed off. When the boys were sure that she was fast asleep, when they heard her snoring, the littlest boy said to the other, "How are we going to kill that big fish? He's a monster of a fish and has killed many people!" The older boy told him, "Well, I don't know of any other way but this: the Sun is my friend, so we'll go up and get some fire from him." The youngest boy spoke again, "But how will we get to where the Sun is?" At that the older boy turned into a raven and turned the younger one into a pigeon. Then he said, "That's the best I can do for you. I cannot turn you into a raven, but I will help you because I can get to where the Sun is. The Sun lives in a big house far across the Big Water. He goes there every night to rest. You, being a pigeon, can't get there, you would fall; but I, being a raven, can help you. Every time you fall I will fly under you and keep you up. That way we can get to where the Sun is."

So, off they flew towards the Sun's house. When they got there, they went inside, but the Sun hadn't come home yet. There was an old woman there who was the Sun's grandmother, and they asked her if the Sun was there. The old woman told them that he had not yet come home, but would be back shortly.

Sure enough, soon the Sun began to appear at his house, coming in with flashes of light. The older boy hid his little brother in the corner behind the door, but the Sun saw him even though he was hidden. Sun asked the older boy, "Who is that?" He answered, "That's our youngest brother." "What did you come here for?" Sun asked. "We came to get some of your fire," the older boy replied. "And what do you want with my fire?" asked Sun. The older boy told Sun, "We need to use it

121

to kill the big fish that is killing many of our people." Sun said, "No, you can't use my fire or you will burn up the Earth — but you can go to my ash pile." So the boys went and got some ashes from the Sun's ash pile and tied them up into very small bundles. Then they took them back to the village.

When they got back they went to the big lake to watch for Xinkwena'mès (the Big Fish). The big fish acted cautiously and kept far away from where they were hidden. Xinkwena'mès was powerful, and knew the intentions of others and could foresee things ahead. So, the boys councilled together and thought of several different ways that they might get near the fish. They thought of using little insects to approach him, and found a pale butterfly to fly near the fish. Xinkwena'mès paid no attention to the butterfly. So the boys decided that the butterfly was the one needed to get near the fish. So, the older boy turned himself into a butterfly and flew around over the water. The other boy dove down into the lake to the center of the Earth and there he emptied out the bundle of ashes he had brought from the Sun. The older boy emptied his ashes as he flew over the water. Then the two boys left and went home. When they got back they lay down in their beds as it wasn't quite daylight yet.

In the morning Grandmother woke up and looked over and saw that the boys were still asleep. So the old woman picked up a wooden stick and began beating the boys, yelling, "Here you are asleep!? You said you were going to kill that Xinkwena'mès!"

The older boy said, "Go out and look at the lake and see what we've done." So Grandmother went there to see for herself, as she didn't believe the boys. When she got to the lake all the water was gone and the big fish was lying from one end of the lake to the other, burnt to a crisp. The ashes from the Sun were so hot that they had dried out the lake and burnt up the fish!

Grandmother found out how the boys killed the fish and she told everyone about it. All the village people went over to where the lake used to be, to see the remains of the big fish.

The wampum was given to the boys for killing Xinkwena'mès, and it is said that those two boys grew to be great men and highly respected by everyone. Some say the oldest became a Chief.

THE WHITE MEN (WAPSITÀK) AND THE BULLOCK'S HIDE

Long ago, before men with white skin had ever been seen upon the Turtle Island, two of our old and wise Lenapé men had a vision, and so they foretold the coming of Wapsini, the White Man. So, they made wampum and laid by the best of their furs to give to them upon their arrival.

One day, some Lenapé men were out fishing, at a place where the sea widens, on what is now called Long Island. In the far distance they saw a strange shape floating on the water, unlike anything they had ever seen before. So, the men immediately took off for home to tell the people of their village about the amazing thing they had just seen. Many people wanted to go back out with them to take a look at the marvel, and so they all hurried out together, and were astonished by what they saw! None of them could agree as to what it was. Some said it was a large fish or animal, and others thought it was a great house floating on the sea. As they watched it, they saw that it was moving towards the land and decided it must be an animal or some other living creature. Then they went back to the village, to tell the Chiefs about what they had seen. Runners and numerous canoes were sent out to carry the news to all of the scattered Chiefs, that they might send off in every direction for warriors, with a message that they should come immediately.

The warriors arrived in great numbers, and having viewed the strange appearance and seeing that it was moving towards the Mahikani Sipu, the Hudson River, said that they thought it must be a remarkably large house in which the Creator himself was present, and that he was probably coming to visit them. By this time the Chiefs had assembled at Manahaxtanànk, York or Manhattan Island, and they councilled among themselves as to how they should greet the Spirit upon his arrival. Every measure was taken to ensure that there was plenty of meat for a feast, and the women went to work preparing the finest foods. All of the sacred bundles and medicines were examined and put in order, and a great dance was planned, to provide the Great Being with an agreeable entertainment and to appease him should he be angry with them for some reason.

The medicine people were consulted, to determine what the coming of this strange appearance might mean and what might result. To the Chiefs and Wise Men of the Nations, men, women and children were looking to for advice and protection. Caught between hope and fear, they were uncertain what to do.

Then fresh runners came, saying that the strange thing was a floating house full of human beings, but of a different color and dressed differently. One of them was said to be dressed all in red and they thought this must be the Great Mànito, the Spirit, himself.

The white people in the floating house called to our Lenape'wàk in a language they did not understand. Many of our people ran off into the woods, but others urged them to stay in order not to give offense to these visitors. The floating house stopped, and a small canoe came ashore with the man dressed in red and some others. Some of them stayed with their canoe to guard it.

The Chiefs and Wise Men assembled in Council, forming themselves in a large circle, towards which the man in red approached with the others. He saluted the Chiefs with a friendly gesture, and the Chiefs told him that they took him by the hand, extending their left hands to shake with him in greeting, as is our ancient custom. He was given wampum and furs as gifts.

The Chiefs were struck with wonder at the dress, manners and appearance of the unknown strangers, and particularly with the man in the red coat with gold trim, which the Chiefs could not account for. They thought he must surely be the Great Mànito, Spirit; but they wondered, "Why should he have a white skin?"

The White Ones then took some liquid which they brought with them and poured it into a cup and gave it to the Chiefs to drink. After drinking first, the Whites handed the liquid first to the Wolf tribe. They drank, and found that it ran towards their hearts and burned their throats. Then it was given to the Turkey tribe who drank, and said to the Whites, "Your health must be very strong!"

The Whites then placed a keg containing this drink on the ground and said to our Chiefs, "Now brethren, we will drink to your health."

Those of the Wolf tribe said to the others, "See what our brothers, the Whites, have given us, that we may drink to their health and to the Great Spirit." For some time many were afraid to drink of it, but then two old men rose and said, "We will partake of this drink, for we are very old and must die soon, so that if this should hasten our deaths it will be no loss to the people."

So, they took the drink and drank it down, and after some time, after many cups, they fell down and their friends thought they had died from the drink. The Chiefs said to each other, "Let each of us go and take a handful of earth from the place where our dead friends lay."

Then they sent for two of their medicine men to go and see whether the two old men were actually dead, so that if they were dead they could bury them with the earth which they were about to take in their hands. The medicine men looked the two men over and told the Chiefs that they were not dead, but in a short time would rise again and shake hands with each other.

After some time the two old men recovered and shook hands. They then went to the Chiefs and told them that they believed the drink of the White brothers possessed good qualities, for they were in excellent health and spirits after their sleep, and had experienced many agreeable sensations from drinking. They then said, "Let's go and see our cousins and thank them for this valuable drink which they have given to us!" Then all the others drank of it also and all became intoxicated.

When their intoxication wore off, the man in red distributed presents among them, beads, axes, hoes and stockings. The Whites soon became familiar with our people and soon learned to speak by signs. They made us understand that they could not stay here, but would return home again and would pay us another visit the following year, when they would bring more presents and stay with us a while; they also told us that, as they could not live without eating, they would like a little land upon which to sow some seeds, in order to raise herbs and crops.

They went away as they had said and returned the next season, and both were happy to see each other; but the Whites laughed at us, seeing that we knew not the use of the axes and hoes they had given to us the year before, for they were hanging around people's necks as ornaments, and the stockings had been put to use as tobacco pouches. The Whites now put handles to the axes, and cut down trees before our eyes, dug up the ground with the hoes, and put the stockings on their legs. A general laughter ensued among our people, as they had been ignorant of the use of such valuable things.

At last the Whites proposed to stay here with us, and asked for enough land for a garden spot; a place, they said, the size of the hide of a bullock. The Chiefs readily granted this apparently reasonable request, and a bullock's hide was spread before them. But then the Whites took a knife, and beginning at one end of the hide, cut it up into a long rope, not thicker than a child's finger, so that by the time it was cut up, it made a great heap. Then they took the rope at one end, and stretched it out, being careful not to break it. It was drawn out into a circle, and it encompassed a large piece of ground. The Chiefs were surprised at the superior wit of the Whites, but did not wish to disagree with them about a little land, as they still had plenty for themselves. We lived together peacefully for a long time, though from time to time the Whites would ask for more land, which was given to them. But they gradually proceeded further and further up Mahikanitàk, the Hudson River (also called Mahikani Sipu), until it began to dawn on we Lenapé that they would soon want all of our country.

And so it proved to be.

* * * * * * * * * * * *

THE WHITE MEN AND THE BULLOCK'S HIDE

This Native version of the coming of the Whites concerns the arrival of Henry Hudson and the Dutch in the Long Island and New York City area.

Of course, the Mahikan and Lenapé association with the Dutch of Manhattan was anything but good. In 1643, in a sign of things still worse to come, the Dutch massacred eighty of our people, men, women and children, after which they stole all of their grain. A war resulted and before hostilities ceased, the Mahikans told the Dutch, "When you first came to our coast, you sometimes had no food. We gave you our beans, corn, oysters, and fish; and now, for recompense, you murder our people. In the beginning of your voyages, you left your people here with goods; we traded with them while your ships were away and cherished them as the apple of our eye. We even gave them our daughters for companions, who have borne children; many Indians have sprung from the Swanekens (Whites). And now, you villainously massacre your own blood!"

GLOSSARY

Algonquin: Native peoples who speak languages similar to the Lenapé, such as the New England tribes, the Ojibwe, the Cree, the Ottawa, Mahican, etc. The Lenapé are considered the grandfathers or progenitors of this group of Native people.

Allegewi: see *Tallegewi*.

Allegewi Sipu: the Ohio River; River of the Allegewi (Tallegewi or Cherokee).

aman'kamèk: a water monster; can also be applied to the horned snakes.

amankaxkti'atmaxkwe, amankaxkwe: the Naked Bear. An ancient animal, now extinct, that attacked and ate people. Its exact identity is unknown.

Amankitaxkwâwikan'ànk: Place of the Great Turtle's Back; the Americas.

api'kân: a flute.

Asiskwàtaja'sàk: the Pleiades; a constellation of stars.

atiloha'kàn: a story that explains natural phenomena, stories of the Spirits, the Creation, etc.

Awâsakàme: the Spirit World, the Land of Souls, the Land Beyond.

axpo'kwès: a mouse.

axsìnamìnshi: the sugar maple tree.

Bikanaki'hàt: another name for the original Water Keeper Spirit — see *Kichichax'kàl*.

chèmà'mès: a rabbit.

chipakwinalitin: the moccasin game, a favorite game among the Native American peoples. Played during a wake for a dead person by we Lenapé; like the pea and shell game.

Chipe'wàk: the Spirits of the Dead, ghosts; sing. *Chipe*.

Clan: a social grouping or designation of people who are descended from a common ancestor.

cradleboard: a board to which a baby was strapped and carried on the mother's back, allowing her to work and watch the child.

enèndàkewa'kàn: a parable, a story that teaches us lessons.

fasting: a process of purification and cleansing, whereby one abstains from food and often water, usually for one to four days. Fasts are undertaken prior to healing and certain religious ceremonies; to

128

concentrate on the spiritual by forgetting our physical bodies.

Guardian Spirit: a Spirit that comes to a person who undergoes a vision (fasting) quest, blessing them, giving them certain powers to help them in their lives and to help their people.

hominy: corn which has been soaked in a solution of water and wood ashes (which makes lye). In the process, the hard, outer hull of the corn seed is loosened and the soft inner part swells, making hominy, which is separated from the loosened corn hulls.

huma: grandmother.

Huma Shawànewànk: Spirit of the South; South Grandmother.

hupa'kàn: a pipe; our sacred, ceremonial pipes were called this also. Pipes were used for invoking spiritual forces and for prayer; also for joining together our minds as one in Council.

Jenkise: the English people; the word *Yankee* is derived from this.

Kahesana Xaskwim: Mother Corn; female spirit of vegetation which gives us food from plants to ensure life.

Keeper Grandmother: a Spirit in the guise of an old woman, who guards the entrance to the Spirit World.

Keepers of Creation: the Spirits of the North, East, South, and West.

kenama'kàn: the giving of thanks, or thanksgiving, at the center of Lenapé religious practice.

Kichichax'kàl: the Great Toad, a Spirit originally given the duty of keeping the waters of the Earth, but who was killed by Maxa'xâk, the horned snake.

Kichiwaxchuwa: the Great, or Rocky Mountains.

kinkinhikàn: a grave marker. They are painted with a sacred red paint called *olàmàn*. A man's marker is a board with a diamond cut at the top, a woman's was a cross with diamonds cut at the ends of the arms.

Kishelamàkânk, -kâng: Lenapé term used for the Creator.

Kishelamìlenk: Lenapé term for the Creator, used when speaking to the Creator, as in prayer.

kishelamàwa'kàn: creation from thought.

klakàptâna'kàn: an amusing or funny story.

ksha'te: tobacco, *Nicotiana rustica*, a Native type of tobacco found in the Americas and grown by our Native people here. *Nicotiana tobaccum*, found in modern day cigarette and tobacco products is milder and native to the Caribbean.

kukhus: an owl.

Kukna: Mother Earth.

kula'kàn: a taboo, or social restriction.

kùna'moxk: an otter.

kwanusa'nèk: a pestle.

Lachimo: a Storyteller, one who traveled around during the winter telling stories. Considered to be bringers of good luck and powerful medicine.

GLOSSARY

lachimosu'wakàn: a story of something in life, past or present.

lachimu: a story.

lachimumenu'tèz: a story bag. A bag containing carved figures or natural objects, each representing a particular story.

lake'in: a clan.

lenapâna: bread made from dried hominy, used to feed those who come to pay their respects upon the death of someone.

Lenapé: our Delaware Indian people, meaning "common people."

leapeâkàn: the Soul or Spirit.

Lenape'hokink, -ing: the eastern homeland of the Lenapé, comprising eastern Pennsylvania, New Jersey, parts of Delaware, the New York City area and southeastern New York state.

Lenapewihìtàk: the Delaware River, meaning "River of the Lenapé."

Lenape'wàk: the Delaware Indian people collectively.

lèpâ'chik: wise men, wise ones. Elders who were looked to for their wisdom and counsel.

linkwehèlan: the vision quest. A fasting quest, alone in the wilderness, whereby one seeks vision relating the path and purpose of one's life, to find one's sacred duty before the Creator and to be of help to one's people. One may also gain thereby a sacred name, medicines, and Guardian Spirits, as well as vision.

Mahalèsànk: Place of Flint, mentioned in the story of Nanapush. Its location is unknown.

Mahicans: see *Mahikani*.

Mahikani: a northern Lenapé people who lived along the Hudson River, north of New York City. Erroneously called the Mohicans.

Mahikani Sipu: the Hudson River.

Mahikanitàk: another name for the Hudson River.

màka'na: a dog.

Manahaxtanànk: Manhattan Island, part of present day New York City.

Mànàka'has: Rainbow Crow. The bringer of fire to the Earth.

Manìto'wàk: Spirit Beings; sing. *Manìto*.

Matantu: Spirit of the Underworld, a complementary, opposing and balancing force to that of the Creator; sometimes destructive, negative and evil.

Maxa'xâk: an evil Spirit Being, Grandfather of the horned serpents or snakes.

maxkwe: a bear.

medicine: a gift of spiritual power. When we talk of medicine we are referring to something spiritual or having spiritual power.

medicine bundle: a bag or bundle, personal or being for a group of people or tribe. Contains natural objects, carvings or animal parts, which confer spiritual power to a person or a people, giving them wisdom, health and well being, good luck, good hunting, protection, etc.

GLOSSARY

Menkwe: the Iroquois Indian people, comprising the Seneca, Cayuga, Onondaga, Oneida, Mohawk and Tuscarora peoples.

Milky Way: a spiral galaxy of which our solar system is but a part, composed of countless stars. Called the Path of Souls, the Star Path, it is the path which the Spirits of the dead travel to reach the Spirit World.

Misinkhâlikàn: a Spirit Being, the Guardian of the Forest and Keeper of the Animals. Known today as Bigfoot or Sasquatch.

mitewile'un: the loon, a northern water bird.

Moontime: a woman's menstrual period.

Munsee, Munsi: a northern division of the Lenapé people, whose homeland was in northern New Jersey and southeastern New York.

Muskanekàm: the Musconetcong mountains of west central New Jersey. The southern reaches of Munsee territory.

Muxumsa Lowànewànk: Spirit of the North; North Grandfather.

Muxumsa Pethakowe: Grandfather Thunder, the Grandfather of the Thunder Beings.

Muxumsa Wapànewànk: Spirit of the East; East Grandfather.

Muxumsa Wunchènewànk: West Grandfather; Spirit of the West.

Namès Sipu: the Mississippi River; lit., "the Fish River."

Nanapush: the Creator's helper and emissary on the Earth. Helper and teacher to humankind.

naxànum: raccoon.

newakishe'na: the four winds.

Nipahuma: Grandmother Moon; lit., "Grandmother who goes by night."

Nishash chak Lèpâ'chik: the Seven Wise men; a term for the Pleiades.

nuchihe'we: a witch.

Nutemahuma: Keeper Grandmother.

Nux Kishux: Father Sun.

olàmàn: a sacred red paint used to paint the face of a deceased person before burial and the grave marker after burial.

pa'kim: a cranberry.

papa'xès: a woodpecker.

pawim: white corn.

Pele: the Turkey clan of the Lenapé people.

Pethakowe'jàk: the Thunderers or Thunder Beings, Spirit helpers of the West that bring the nourishing rains to all life and warnings to humankind.

pimâ'kàn: a sweatlodge or sweatlodge ceremony, used for cleansing/purification of the body, heart, mind and Spirit.

Pimikishika'tèk: the Path of Souls, the Milky Way.

Poko'unko, -ungo: the Turtle clan of the Lenapé people.

red cedar: *Juniperus virginiana*; an evergreen tree whose leaves and wood are used for purifying places of evil influences and in smudging people. The wood is very aromatic.

131

GLOSSARY

sage: aromatic herbs of the *Salvia* species, used for smudging and purifying.

Sakimâ: a Chief.

san'kwe: a weasel.

sàpan: hot cereal made from cornmeal.

sèsapink: blue corn.

shikak: a skunk.

sisawin: an oyster.

smudging: a purification done with the smoke from burning certain aromatic herbs and trees. A feather is used to direct the smoke over a person's body or an object.

sukaxkuk chipik: black snake root, an herb; *Cimicifuga racemosa*.

takwiphâtin: a funeral feast.

Tallegewi, Tàlekewi: our name for the people we encountered northeast of the Mississippi River in our ancient migrations. Probably the Tsalagi or Cherokee people.

tamakwa: a beaver.

tamask'was: a muskrat.

tàme: a wolf.

tàme'tut: a coyote.

taxkwâx: the turtle, carried the new Earth on its back.

Taxkwâx Mènâ'te: Turtle Island; another name for the Americas.

taxoxi kowàni'kàn: a turtle shell rattle; a sacred rattle used for healing and in special ceremonies. Not used in social music.

tèsamana'ne: a high energy food made from roasted blue corn meal; used as food by warriors and hunters, as it could be easily carried and a little went a long way.

Tinde Wulankuntowa'kàn: the Fire of Peace; the sacred fire made for Councils and ceremonies as taught to us by Nanapush.

titàs: the downy woodpecker.

tobacco: see *ksha'te*.

Tuksit: the Wolf clan of the Lenapé people.

Unalaxtako: a division of our Lenapé people who lived along the New Jersey coast and in southern New Jersey.

Unami: a division of our Lenapé people who lived along the Delaware River and its tributaries.

Unextako: the Nanticoke people, close relatives of the Lenapé, living in Delaware, Maryland, and Virginia.

ulikwàn: the flicker; a bird closely related to the woodpecker.

vision quest: see *linkwehèlan*.

wampum: beads made from conch shells and certain clams, white or black in color, considered sacred and used to bind agreements and treaties before the Creator.

Wapalanìto: the Spirit helper of the East, messenger between this world and the Spirit World.

GLOSSARY

wapink: an opossum.

Wapsitàk: White People; sing. *Wapsini*, *Wapsit*.

Wèhixamu'kès: Lenapé legendary figure; said to come back someday to our people, bringing back our culture and traditions.

Wematekàn'is: the Little People of the forest; Earth Spirits who help Misinkhâlikàn.

white cedar: evergreen trees of the *Thuja* species, with aromatic, flat leaves.

wihunge: an annual memorial feast held in honor of a deceased person.

wiktut: a menstrual lodge.

wikwàm: a house.

winke'màsk: sweetgrass; an aromatic grass with a vanilla-like odor that is burned to call up good Spirits and used for smudging.

Wunchène'kis: another name for Muxumsa Wunchènewànk, or West Grandfather.

xapânkwe: ears of corn braided by the husks and hung up to dry.

xaskwim: corn.

Xinkwelenowàk: Giants.

Xinkwikàn: our old Lenapé Big House ceremony. It was held in the fall and lasted for twelve days.

yakwawi: the mastodon, a prehistoric elephant.

BIBLIOGRAPHY

R. C. Adams, *Legends of the Delaware Indians and Picture Writing.* Washington, D.C., 1905.

Daniel G. Brinton, *The Lenapé and Their Legends.* Philadelphia, 1884.

Clarence Chamberlain, Private Journals. Unpublished.

M. R. Harrington, *Religion and Ceremonies of the Lenapé.* New York, 1921.

Rev. John Heckewelder, *History, Manners, and Customs of the Indian Nations.* Philadelphia, 1876.

Indianapolis, Indiana Historical Society, *Walam Olum or Red Score, the Migration Legend of the Lenni Lenape or Delaware Indians, a New Translation.* Indianapolis, 1954.

Truman Michelson, *Ethnological and Linguistic Field Notes from the Munsee in Kansas and the Delaware in Oklahoma.* Smithsonian Archives, 1912.

Frank G. Speck, *Oklahoma Delaware Ceremonies, Feasts, and Dances.* Philadelphia, 1937.

C. A. Weslager, *The Delaware Indian Westward Migration.* Middle Atlantic Press, Wallingford, Pa., 1978.